Fae Child

Jane-Holly Meissner

Published by Inkshares, Inc., Oakland, California
www.inkshares.com

Edited by Avalon Radys
Cover illustration and design by Aliana Wong
Interior design by Kevin G. Summers

ISBN: 9781950301171
e-ISBN: 9781950301188
Library of Congress Control Number: 2020947102

First edition

Printed in the United States of America

for Owen, Sophie, Olivia, and Logan
be strong and courageous

CHAPTER 1

Through the Pond

ABIGAIL D. BROWN was like most other eight-year-old girls: creative, inquisitive, and precocious, though perhaps taller than some. She spent most of her summers exploring the woods behind her house. Her mother called it a *green space*, but to Abbie it was the *forest*, and if you called a forest by any other name, it lost some of its inherent magic.

The early summer day began with a rainstorm that blanketed the town in a thick humidity unusual for Oregon. By midday, the humidity had burned off, giving way to the sort of dry heat that singes bare feet on stone pathways baking in the sun. Abbie sat on a mossy stump, watching gold-fuzzed bees swarm the petite white blooms of a blackberry bramble, and she anticipated the bountiful harvest she'd enjoy in the coming months. Picking berries and eating them until her fingers and lips (and clothes, to her mother's private horror) stained purple was one of her favorite things about summer.

Abbie was often alone (if you don't count her parents' company), but she didn't mind. She had friends among the other kids in the neighborhood, but she tended toward solitary flights of fancy, playing with her dog, and scribbling stories in a battered notebook in her large, childish handwriting. The other children seemed to prefer playing video games and watching other people play video games on the internet. Abbie's parents didn't have the internet or a television in their house. Her father homeschooled her, which meant she could focus on subjects that interested her. Dan, her father, brought her outside to enjoy their lessons in the fresh air when the weather was fine. Of course, the Oregon weather was often dreary or cloudy, but bundling up in raincoats and splashing about in mud puddles was almost as fun as running barefoot in the woods during the summer.

Abbie looked down at her dirty toes and wiggled them. If they were here, Mom would make her put her sandals back on (in case she stepped on something sharp), but Dad would wink and tell her to enjoy herself. After a few moments of toe wiggling, she slipped her flip-flops back on and stood up. The bees buzzed around her as she meandered past the tangle of thorny vines into a mass of tall clover growing under enormous fir trees. "C'mon, Sammy," she called.

Sammy, her little Jack Russell terrier, bounded out of the bushes and nearly took her out at the knees. Abbie knelt and ruffled his ears.

"Who's a good booooy," she crooned, and Sammy wagged his tail and licked her face, much to her delight. "You're all dirty!" she cried, fending off his licks. "C'mon, I'm hungry. Let's get something to eat." Sammy barked, turning a quick circle in his excitement.

She pressed her hand to her stomach as it rumbled and looked up through the trees at the blue sky. The sun was well overhead, which meant it was close to noon. Abbie picked up the pace, running down her trail toward her hidden lunchbox, with Sammy at her heels. She'd stashed it in the cool, dark shadow of a fallen log, and she brushed off the dirt as she pulled it out. Sammy sat patiently, waiting for her to decide where they would be eating.

She sat on the log, opening her lunch as she decided that it was as good a place as any, when the trees seemed to spin around her. Abbie dropped her lunchbox as she put her hands out to balance herself and gasped at her sudden unsteadiness. The ground lurched, tipping to one side as though the world was trying to throw her off the log, and she had the sensation that if she let go of her perch, she would be swept away. Unaffected by this phenomenon, Sammy lunged at the spilled lunch, scarfing down the scattered dog biscuits where they lay among the leaves. A wave of nausea nearly overwhelmed Abbie, and then the forest settled, seeming to straighten itself, no longer trying to pitch her to the ground or spin her like a top. She managed to focus on Sammy as he angled to move on to her sandwich once he had finished the biscuits.

She put her foot out to block him. "No! Bad dog!"

Sammy backed up, looking as contrite as a dog could while chewing a mouthful of ill-gotten treats. Abbie dropped to her knees in the dirt, blowing the forest detritus off her sandwich as best she could before repacking her lunchbox.

"What was that, Sammy? Did you feel it?" As she spoke, Abbie could *still* feel that something bizarre was happening around her in the forest, though the effect was far less pronounced than it had been a moment before. It felt as if a thousand butterflies were pressing against her in every direction, but from the inside of her body.

Sammy nuzzled her hands, looking for more biscuits. Abbie pushed him away, stood up, and brushed leaves off her knees. "I feel . . . tingly." She looked in the direction of home, somewhere beyond the trees in front of her, and then to the right, where the strange spinning, fluttery feeling seemed to emanate from. She didn't know *how* she knew that, she just *did*, as if she were a scientist charting the epicenter of an earthquake.

"C'mon, Sammy," she said, darting off the path toward the strangeness. Strange meant new, new meant exciting, and exciting meant she'd have a good story to tell her dad when she got home. He loved her stories.

Abbie slowed down, making her way carefully through the ferns and forest clover. Now she was off the well-traveled path. Where she was didn't look familiar, but it *felt* right, as if she'd been there before. In Abbie's experience, running off into new places could mean scraping through a load of thorns, so she was careful, but she was also curious, and curiosity was at the heart of any exploration or new adventure. Sammy barked warningly as she edged past a large purple foxglove, and she shushed him.

"Be brave, Sammy," she told her dog. He whined but obediently followed her into the clearing.

A beautiful pond lined with lush ferns and a drooping willow tree on its bank lay in front of them. Wildflowers in all the colors Abbie could imagine were sprinkled throughout the clearing, and the sun shone down through the gap in the trees, reflecting brilliantly off the smooth water.

"Look!" she cried with delight, picking her way through the flowers. Sammy excitedly chased a butterfly, paying no attention to her whatsoever. Abbie emerged from the knee-deep wildflowers at the edge of the pond and peered down at the smooth stones she could see through the clear water.

"Maybe there's fish!" she called out to Sammy, but he ignored her still, jumping after the fluttering insect but missing every time.

Abbie left her flip-flops at the edge of the pond and waded barefoot into the cool water, her lunch still clutched in her hand. She didn't see any fish, just rounded pebbles. She was careful not to go deeper than her shins.

"C'mon, Sammy!" she called, turning around to look for him. Instead, she caught sight of something reflecting in the water by the edge of the pond. A boy!

Abbie looked up, startled, her eyes searching for him, but he must have pulled back into the ferns. She took a slow step back toward the bank, looking back at the water where she'd seen the boy's face—and there he was again! "Hey, come back!" she called, sloshing over toward him. "Stop hiding!"

The boy looked surprised as she accidentally splashed water, disturbing his reflection, but he didn't move much, except to look closer at the surface of the pool.

Abbie stopped wading, looking at the empty spot on land where he should have been crouched, and then back to the reflection where she could clearly see him.

"How do you do that?" she said, amazed. "Are you underwater?" The boy said nothing. He just stared back. He appeared to be a few years older than her, and he was wearing green clothes.

Sammy leapt into the pond behind Abbie, splashing and barking happily. She grabbed his collar with her hand, maintaining a grip on her lunchbox under her arm.

"Shusssh," she murmured, reaching down toward the face.

Her hand cut into the water, and the boy drew back, alarmed, but she still couldn't see where he was on the bank.

"Don't go!" Abbie called, "Please!" She dipped her hand in up to her elbow, but she couldn't feel the stones she knew must be there because she was standing on them. Abbie waved her hand underwater even though Sammy was pressing against her leg, about to knock her over headfirst into the water. Mom would be mad that she was all wet, but this was probably the weirdest thing that had ever happened to her in her entire life.

Abbie shrieked as a hand clutched hers and yanked her down into the pond. Sammy barked, trying to pull her back, and slipped out of his collar. She couldn't breathe, the water pressing in around her tightly as she was pulled deeper and deeper.

She struggled to get free, desperate for air, but the boy's grip was forceful. The world spun around her, sending tingles up and down her spine. It felt as if she was caught in a whirlpool; she couldn't tell which way was up anymore. Finally, her head burst through the surface, and she gasped for air, her lunchbox popping up and floating away from her as she flailed her arms, finally knocking away the grasping hand as she tried to get her feet back underneath her. The water was much, much deeper than she'd thought, and it took a moment for her to realize she needed to be swimming rather than trying to stand.

"Where have you come from?" called a boy's voice. Abbie blinked wildly through water-filled eyes, struggling to concentrate on the boy braced on the bank, reaching out to her again. "Take my hand!"

Desperate, Abbie slapped her hand into his, and he pulled her to the bank, where she collapsed onto the ferns. She was still clutching Sammy's collar, but the dog was nowhere to be seen. She looked up at the sun, shielding her eyes from its brightness, and then she sat up abruptly. "Why did you pull me in?"

"Why did I—I pulled you out!" The boy crouched out of arm's reach, his blond hair curly and messy. His face was dirty, Abbie noticed, and his clothes were... well, they looked like leaves. She knew it wasn't polite to stare, so she turned her attention to finding Sammy. She stuck her fingers between her lips to whistle for him.

The boy clapped his hands over his ears, his eyes wide as Abbie frowned and repeated her whistle.

"How did you do that?" he asked.

"It's just a whistle," Abbie said, a little self-consciously. "Like this." She put two fingers back into her mouth and tried to show him how she was holding her tongue. "Like between your teeth, but kinda behind them."

He leaned forward, fascinated, but quickly retreated when she unleashed another piercing whistle. "You're gonna have the wolves on top of us if you keep doing that!" He grabbed her wrist and pulled her hand away from her mouth.

"There aren't any wolves around here," she said, matter-of-factly. "Anyway, *you* asked!"

"I didn't know you were going to do it again," he protested.

"Well, I didn't know you were going to pull me into the water! That's pretty rude." Abbie frowned at him. Where was Sammy? He usually came running when she whistled for him.

"You were in the water already! And your hand came out!" The boy put his hand up in the air, waving it about. "I helped you!"

"No, you pulled me in," she said, pouting a little. "And now I'm all wet." Abbie bunched up the front of her yellow T-shirt and wrung out as much water as she could. Her denim shorts would just have to stay wet...and she'd lost her sandals. "What's your name, anyway?"

"Foster," he said, cautiously watching her try to squeeze the water out of her shoulder-length brown hair. "What's your name?"

"Abbie. Abigail, really," she replied. She stuck her hand out to shake, and he peered at it for a moment before taking it and giving it a tentative squeeze. Foster dropped her hand quickly. Abbie grinned at him but then frowned as she looked properly around.

"Where did all the trees go? Did you see my dog?" For a panicked moment she wondered if Sammy was still in the water, and she turned and waded back into the lake.

The weeping willow tree and the wildflowers were still in place, but the meadow had suddenly become much larger. The towering evergreens of her forest had fallen away, and instead maple trees grew in the distance.

"The trees are where they have been," said Foster, unhelpfully, watching her splash her hands in the water. "Come back! You cannot return that way!"

"No they aren't!" Abbie straightened, turning in a circle in the pond. "They're all wrong. Those aren't my trees."

"No, they aren't anyone's trees," said Foster, standing up. "They own themselves."

She stared at him incredulously. "Trees can't own anything. They're trees."

He frowned. "Exactly."

Abbie matched his expression. "What?" She paused and then yelled, "Sammy!" Where had he gone?

"I'm going home now." She looked around, feeling a little scared for the first time. "Once I find my dog." Abbie sloshed back out of the pond and started toward the tree line opposite the willow tree, roughly the way she'd entered the clearing.

Foster darted forward, standing in front of her as she started to walk away toward the maple trees. "Wait! You were both in the pond. I think I might have—I mean, I didn't, but it's the only thing that makes sense."

She stamped her foot down in frustration. "You aren't making any sense!"

"I was playing," he said. "Practicing."

Foster scratched his head, pushing his wildly curly hair behind his ears. Abbie stared at them, her mouth falling open into a small *O*.

"Your ears are pointy," she interrupted, rudely.

"Oh! Oh, yes, they are." Foster moved closer, peering at her, and she took a step back, stumbling over a hidden rock. "Is everyone like you where you live?"

Abbie caught herself and put her hands firmly on her hips.

"No one is like me. And who are you, and why am I here, and where is *here*?" Her voice got louder with every word, and Foster put his finger to his lips.

"Sssh!" He looked around wildly. "I was using my magic, of course. I'm a guardian of the forest. Well, I will be, and I was practicing. Just little spells, but I've seen the gate spell done before, from far away, and it's similar enough to—" he looked at Abbie's wild eyes and hurried on. "But that does not matter. I saw you in the water and then your hand came out." He began to grimace as he spoke, as if the full gravity of what he'd done was finally sinking in. "I pulled you though. If your dog was with you, he must have been left behind."

"Left behind where?" asked Abbie, looking behind her at the pond. A fish broke the surface, its mouth gaping for a moment before it slipped back under. "The water?"

"Through the gate. Into the Otherworld." Foster took a step back, arms spread in apology. "Uh, sorry?"

CHAPTER 2

Meet the Fairies

CHILDREN TEND TO embrace the world around them as they experience it—with wonder and delight at each new discovery. An adult may view dandelions as nothing more than pesky weeds; to the young, they are golden flowers that greet the sun and hide from the night, transforming as if by magic into wishflowers that can be blown into the wind. Everything is new, and anything can be celebrated.

When told that she was in another world, however, Abbie did not react with joy and delight. She stamped her foot.

"Take me back home right now!" she bellowed at the boy with the pointed ears.

"I cannot!" he exclaimed, reaching for her hand. She pulled away from him, splashing backward into the water for a third time. The boy grimaced, as if bracing himself for her wrath.

"If the pond is a gate, then I'm going back home," Abbie fumed. She used her meanest voice to hide her growing fear. "You're going to help me!"

Foster shook his head emphatically. "Oh, no. No! I cannot help you. The Queen watches—I mean, she probably already knows you are here—but she watches *the Gate*." As he spoke, he gave the word a subtle emphasis that indicated this Gate had a capital letter and was important. "You cannot go back though an unsanctioned gate."

Foster's knees buckled, and he collapsed into the ferns, the color draining from his tanned face.

Abbie bit her lip, growing more worried because of the boy's expression. She splashed back to dry land, flopping down next to Foster, her pond-soaked clothes squishing underneath her. He covered his face with his hands, and she sighed unhappily.

"What did you mean by an, uh, 'un-sank-shunned' gate?"

"A portal opened beyond the ken or purview of the Queen," said Foster, his words muffled by his hands. He looked through his fingers at her, saw the look on her face, and lifted his head. "Gates are controlled by the Queens. You are not allowed to open one unless you are granted permission."

"Can't I just go back through?" Abbie wished Sammy was there to hug for comfort. She glanced hopefully around the meadow once more.

"No. Well, you could," Foster conceded. "I would have to open it again, but I am not really sure how I did it in the first place. And on top of that," he added, "going through a gate without the blessing of the Fae, to return home... you could end up a hundred years in the future in your world. It is a tricky magic and I am not good enough, even if I were allowed to do it. And I am not."

Abbie glowered, her brows knit together as she looked away from the older boy, across the pond.

"How do I get home, then?" Before he could answer, she rounded on him. "You brought me here; you have to help me get back. You're responsible for me."

"I am," Foster agreed, though he looked a little green at the thought. "You *could* return to the world through the main Gate, in the Queen's Palace, in the center of Summer. Otherworld is divided into Summer and Winter—"

"Like Fairyland?" interrupted Abbie. "I've read fairy stories before… is that—is this where I am? The Fairy Kingdom?" He'd mentioned the Fae, but it hadn't clicked until now. "Summer's Queen is Tita—ow!" Foster clapped his hand over her mouth before she could finish, silencing her with terror in his eyes.

"Do not speak her name! You will draw her eyes!"

Abbie stared at him, her own eyes wide.

"Okay," she said, pulling his hand from her face. "Sheesh, sorry." She looked around them with new appreciation.

Foster smoothed down his leaf shirt, his eyes a little wild.

"The Gate you need is in the center of Summer, and this is the height of her power. You will not get there unseen, and if you are found…"

Abbie waited for him to finish, but it appeared he already had. "…if I'm found… what? Won't…won't she let me go home?" Her lower lip trembled.

"*Maybe* she would," said Foster, lowering his voice to a sad whisper. "But it will be over my dead body." It wasn't a threat, just a plain, sad fact. "More likely she will make you one of her servants, to serve her forever and ever. And ever and ever and ever," he continued, as he lay down in the ferns and stared up at the blue sky. Abbie thought she saw doom in his eyes.

She reached over and grabbed him by the shoulders, shaking him. "We can't just sit here, waiting for her to find us!" Abbie pressed to her feet. "You did it once already—maybe you can learn how to do it again, and, like, not send me a zillion years into the future."

Foster sat up. "It takes years to master one's magic!"

"Well, I'm not staying here," said Abbie. She marched off toward the tree line again, bees flying up from the wildflowers as she waded through them.

"You do not know where you are going," Foster called plaintively after her.

The girl didn't stop, continuing her stubborn, barefoot walk. Foster sighed, pushed himself to his feet, and ran after her. Catching up, he said, "Wait! You are heading toward a far darrig's territory."

Abbie stopped walking, narrowing her eyes. "A what? Are they nice?"

"Far darrig. The red caps. And no, not even to other red caps," Foster said.

"Are you a fairy?" she asked abruptly, turning to him.

"No, fairies are *little*," he said, indignantly. "I am an elf. Guardian of the forest, remember?"

Abbie frowned, trying to think, but her thoughts hopped all over the place.

"My dad is really smart. I bet he can find a way to get me home...?" Foster shook his head. "No?"

"Your parents will not even know you are gone," he said. "Old magic, some of the oldest, is woven into the Gate spell. Those who stumble through from their world into ours," he said, sounding as if he was reading from a textbook, "are copied in body but not soul, leaving a changeling in their stead. The changeling is just like the person they have replaced, but—" he stopped abruptly to glance at her before changing tack and continuing. "They are like a... reflection of you. Since you are not gone, your parents will not look for you."

Foster's face brightened. "But you can stay with me. You are right; I am responsible for you. And there are other humans here, too! You will like it here." He jumped out in front of her, blocking her way. "You will not like it with the far darrig. They are not too close, but… probably best to go a different direction." He hesitated, studying her face. "Why are you crying? Do not cry!"

"I'm not crying." Abbie sniffed, a big, fat tear rolling off the tip of her nose. "I just wanna go home, and you're confusing me."

"Come on," he said, pulling the human girl close in an awkward hug. "I will show you something that will make you happy. But stop crying first." Foster looked around worriedly as Abbie sobbed into his leafy shirt. "Tears might attract the Wee Folk, and then we will have no end of nonsense. We have enough trouble already. Please?"

She nodded, his shirt surprisingly soft against her damp cheek, then pushed away from him.

"O-o-okay," Abbie quavered, wiping her eyes.

Foster smiled encouragingly and began leading them westward. He looked all around them as they walked—was that a flicker of tiny wings behind them? *Just my imagination.* He willed it to be so, and took her hand, pulling her along into the shade of the trees.

"What kind of magic do you do?" she asked, following him because she didn't know what else to do.

"Forest magic," he said, picking up the pace. "Do you always ask so many questions?"

"Yes?" Abbie said, struggling to keep up with the elven boy. "Especially when I meet an elf in the woods for the first time in my whole life, and I end up in Fairyland, and—"

"Fair enough," he interrupted, practically towing her along behind him. "Oh, no."

"Oh, no?" She bumped into him when he stopped abruptly to look around. All she saw were trees and some dragonflies. Abbie felt a pang of fear at the thought of leaving the pond—her only connection to back home and her parents. She realized she'd been holding her breath.

"Wee Folk," Foster groaned, picking a daisy from the forest floor and turning to face the dragonflies.

Abbie's mouth fell open as she realized the dragonflies weren't insects at all, but tiny people with translucent wings. They flitted between the trees, the dappled sunlight reflecting from their iridescent clothes. Foster pulled her behind him, brandishing the flower like a rapier.

"I wanna see," she complained. "Are those fairies?"

"Unfortunately," her companion said. "They are attracted to wild emotions and curiosity. We may never be rid of them if you keep asking questions."

Abbie ducked to peek out from under his armpit as the largest of the little fairies drew near. He held a twig in his hand and wore an adorable acorn hat.

"Is that cherry?" Foster muttered, but then pronounced, "Halt! I am a Guardian and you may not harass me or my charge!"

The fairy hovered like a hummingbird, his wings buzzing as he regarded the two creatures in front of him.

"I am Table," he proclaimed regally, his voice small but not high pitched. "We only wish to play. Put away your flower!"

"Put away your stick," replied Foster. "Do not think I do not know what it is."

Five or six other fairies had clustered around the first, and Abbie watched them with wonder.

Table drew himself up to his full height of about eight inches. "I will not release my staff. Why, you might as well ask me to cut off my arm! But your flower, you will not need it."

"I like this flower," retorted the elf. He raised it a little higher in warning as one of the Wee Folk looked about to flank him. They reconvened into a single group, settling in the lower branches of the nearest tree.

Abbie giggled. "Is your name really Table?"

"Abbie!" said Foster, exasperated. "Do not encourage them."

"My name is Table, indeed, fair maiden," said the fairy, giving her a bow from his spot in the tree. "This is Fork, Door, Roof, Curtain, and Rug." Each of the fairies bowed in turn.

"They are not allowed inside," said Foster. "Over time, the Wee Folk have become overly fascinated with things found inside houses."

"I think they're cute," said Abbie.

"They are pests," Foster said. "They will be starting with riddles soon, and—no, that was not an invitation!" he shouted as Table perked up at the mention of word games.

"We only want to play," said Fork, or maybe it was Rug. The fairy turned a cartwheel and Abbie clapped with delight while Foster sagged, realizing he would no doubt lose this fight. Perhaps they could escape the Wee Folk before day turned to night, though it appeared the fairy magic had already taken effect, turning even his thoughts into a rhyming dialect.

"Stop that!" he said, "You are an annoying little gnat."

"Foster," Abbie protested, but whatever she was going to say was lost as a wolf howl pierced through the forest. The fairies scattered like leaves in the wind.

A second howl echoed the first from a different direction. Foster handed Abbie the daisy.

"You are going to need this."

He grabbed her hand, and they started running.

CHAPTER 3

Incursion

SHE MUST BE running late. Dan Brown looked at the lengthening shadows in the backyard and leaned on the back fence. "Abbie!" he called into the trees, listening for the telltale sounds of Sammy or for his daughter's voice calling after the pup.

There was no reply.

After the brief, startled silence left by his worried calls, the birds began to sing again. Dan narrowed his green eyes, his hand on the gate. Abbie was always home when he asked her to be.

"Is something wrong?"

Dan looked over his shoulder to his wife standing at the back door of their two-story house and smiled.

"She's just a little late," he said, as if to reassure himself.

"I wish you wouldn't let her run wild like that," Fiona fussed, stepping out into the vanishing sunlight and crossing the grass. "How late is she?" She worked her hands through her long blond hair as she spoke, pulling it into a low ponytail.

"Just a little bit." He pulled her close and kissed her cheek while she finished fussing with her hair, and she laughed. "I hate that you have to go to work right now."

"Babies only come on their own schedules," she said, pushing him away with a grin. "You'll call me if she—oh, there she is."

"Being on call is surely the worst invention of mankind," agreed Dan, turning to look where Fiona was pointing. Abbie waved, walking down the path toward them between the trees, and he waved back.

"It comes with the territory," she said, straightening her button-up shirt and slacks. "I'll call you later. I'm expecting an uncomplicated delivery. Hey, sweetie," she added, scooping Abbie up into a hug as the girl opened the gate. "One of my patients is going into labor, so it'll be a late night. I love you, and I'll see you later, okay?"

"Okay, Mom," said Abbie, hugging her mother tightly. Dan smiled at the sight and then looked with concern back into the forest.

"Where's Sammy?"

Fiona put Abbie down, rubbing her nose to her daughter's. "Be good for your dad."

"Always," grinned Abbie, clinging to Fiona a little longer. "I wish you didn't have to go!"

"Abbie, where is Sammy?" asked Dan, a little more urgently.

"I...don't know," replied Abbie, looking back. Her little brow creased with concern.

"Oh dear," grimaced Fiona. "You've got this, right?"

"Of course," said Dan. "Have a good night." She gave him a quick peck on the lips before hurrying back into the house to grab her things, and he returned his attention to his daughter. "Where was he when you last saw him?"

"It was just a little while ago!" Abbie's brown eyes welled up with tears. "Where is he?"

"It'll be fine," Dan said. "Sammy probably just followed an interesting smell and wandered off. Let's go look for him."

"O-okay," she sniffled, putting her little hand in his. Walking through the gate back into the green space, Dan gave her fingers a squeeze, which she reciprocated. "Do you think he's lost?" Abbie asked, her voice still quavering as she tried not to cry.

"Sammy is a smart dog," Dan reassured her, while he looked around with concern, resisting the parental urge to ask why she hadn't paid more attention to him. "He just likes to chase squirrels. Where were you walking today?"

"Just out where we usually are," she said, clutching his hand. Abbie wasn't usually this clingy, and Sammy certainly was never this quiet. Dan whistled loudly, but no happy barks came in reply.

After following the trail through the fir trees for about half an hour, he finally made the tough decision to go home.

"We'll make some posters," Dan said, hugging Abbie close. "One of the neighbors will see him. It'll be okay."

Dinner was a quiet affair. Abbie stared at her plate with red-rimmed eyes and pushed her broccoli around with her fork. He didn't press her into finishing, silently cursing Sammy and his need for freedom that was causing his daughter so much pain. When she asked to be excused, he let her go, and she ran upstairs while he gathered up their plates and the silverware.

He found her later in her bed, covers pulled up to her chin. "Are you okay, Abbie?"

Dan put his hand on her hair, then moved it to her forehead. She felt a little warm, but she was tucked in tightly for a summer night. He pulled on the comforter, loosening it around her.

"Worried about Sammy?"

"Yes," she said after a moment, looking into his eyes. "But pretty tired, too, Daddy."

"I thought we could do a poster to put up in the neighborhood," he said. She looked away toward the wall. "It's not your bedtime yet, if you want to help me?" He adjusted the comforter and felt the hard shapes of her shoes under the covers. Dan frowned and pulled the covers down. "Why are you wearing your dirty clothes in your bed?"

Abbie sat up, looking down at herself.

"I... don't know."

She swung her legs out of bed, and then stood up, standing there for a minute while he brushed her sheets with his hand to make sure they were clean.

"Come on. Let's get your teeth brushed and pajamas on." Dan pushed himself off the floor and stepped over to her dresser. She quickly followed him, taking his hand and resting her head on his arm. He gave her a strange look, detached her from his hand, and pulled her Tinkerbell nightgown from the top drawer, helping her into it.

Once Abbie was back in her bed, he went through the motions of making a Lost Dog poster, carefully hand lettering it and picking a few photographs of Sammy for Abbie to choose from for the final product. He found himself looking up at the ceiling a few times, up to where he knew Abbie was sleeping in her pajamas. He'd felt something when she'd hugged his hand... something strange.

Dan fell asleep while reading a book in bed, making a futile effort to stay awake until Fiona got back from the hospital. He woke up hours later, his wife curled up with her back to him, her blond hair fanned out on her pillow. Sitting up and putting his book on the nightstand, he leaned over to give her a kiss—and saw Abbie snuggled in her mother's arms, sleeping soundly. He straightened and hesitantly put his hand on Fiona's shoulder before withdrawing as if he'd stuck his finger in the electrical socket. Dan gave Abbie's unconscious form a sharp look, then carefully climbed out of bed, padding out of the room and down the stairs barefoot.

In the kitchen, he picked up the phone, cradling the receiver against his ear while he dialed a number he'd memorized long ago but hoped to never use. While he waited for the call to connect, he looked at the time. Could he expect someone to answer at three in the morning?

A scratch at the sliding door caught his attention, and he looked up to see Sammy standing in the starlight, black nose against the seam of the door. He made eye contact with the mud-clad Jack Russell just as the call connected.

"State your business." The male voice on the other end sounded like he'd pounded three espressos right before picking up the phone.

Dan took a deep breath. "I need to speak to the Cat."

There was a long silence, long enough for Dan to wonder if he'd been hung up on, and then the man said, "Credentials?"

"Tell her it's Wodan." He paused, looking up at the ceiling with worry in his eyes. "I've got an incursion."

CHAPTER 4

Farther In

THE HOWLS SOUNDED closer, their haunting calls bouncing off the trees, but Abbie was more concerned with keeping up with Foster as he dashed through the forest, clutching her by the hand. She wanted to look behind, to see what might be chasing them, but she was afraid she would trip and fall if she took her eyes away from the boy.

She wanted to ask *so* many questions, but Foster held her hand in a vice grip, and she was soon dragging deep gulps of air into her lungs as she did her best to keep up. Tree branches loomed overhead, their dense canopy casting the ground in shadow as they grew closer and closer together, the way ahead becoming less clear.

As Foster pulled her straight toward an enormous oak tree, Abbie shrieked, trying desperately to free herself from his grip as he sped up. At the last moment, he waved his free hand, the tree trunk splitting silently lengthwise and opening like a wardrobe as the two children tumbled inside.

She gaped up at the crack of forest light before it disappeared, leaving them in complete darkness.

"What—" she started, her voice thin and high pitched as she pulled her knees up in front of her, but Foster shushed her.

After a moment, a warm orange glow enveloped the elf's hand, coalescing into a small flame. Abbie wrapped her arms around her knees as she took in her surroundings. Sitting inside a tree was nothing like she might have imagined, had she ever considered it before. The room, if that's what she could call it, was egg-shaped with polished wood walls and floor and just enough room for them to sit inside it. She opened her mouth to talk again, and Foster shook his head, his blond curls falling into his eyes.

"They are close," he said, so softly she could barely hear him. The flame on his palm shrunk until it was just a tiny thing, and she stared at it, fascinated.

How is he doing that? Is he holding a candle? Abbie leaned forward to get a better look and then peeked under Foster's hand. There was nothing, only the small bit of fire inexplicably burning in his hand. Foster looked at her, and then toward where they had entered the tree, placing a finger against his lips.

Abbie frowned, listening intently just as a wolf's howl tore through the air outside their hideaway. Startled, she jumped, her hand tightening on Foster's arm. She was still clutching the daisy Foster had given her, and when she focused past it, she realized that she'd skinned her knee falling into the tree. Once noticed, the scrape suddenly became painful, and her eyes welled up with tears.

Foster's eyes tightened as he followed her tearful gaze to a drop of blood beading on her knee. Heavy footsteps padded the ground close by as whatever had been pursuing them seemed to pause, investigating the area outside the tree thoroughly. Foster brought his finger to his lips once more, and Abbie nodded, lips trembling and eyes wide.

The moments stretched into minutes, but the tree was surprisingly comfortable as she leaned back against the curved interior. The scrape on her knee faded to a dull ache as the footsteps receded and the howling became more distant. She watched Foster, who was crouched where they had entered the tree, turn his head this way and that as he listened. The flame in his hand danced and turned green before he dismissed it, pressing his palm to the smooth wood in the sudden darkness.

The wolves had moved on, though with no trail to follow, they would likely double back. As the tree opened to release them from its protection, Foster cautiously poked his head outside.

"They are gone," he said with relief, pushing himself up and reaching down to help Abbie to her feet.

She stepped out of the tree, looking back at the hidey-hole with wonder.

"How did you . . . what was that? Why are wolves chasing us?"

She backed away from the large oak as it began to close, bumping into another tree trunk. She stared at Foster and then sagged against the smaller tree, suddenly drained.

"Because you are not meant to be here, and I certainly was not supposed to bring you here. Wolves work for the Queen. They always have . . . " His voice trailed off helplessly, his eyes flitting back and forth quickly, as if parsing through disjointed thoughts. "They must have sensed the gate opening and trailed us from the pond."

"Are we safe now?"

Abbie rested her chin on one knee and tried, to no avail, to resist poking at the scrape on the other.

"For now. I disguised our scent, and the oak hid us well enough." He rotated as he spoke, studying their surroundings.

"Well, that's good," she said, her eyes lighting up.

"They will return," he cautioned. "To pick up the trail again."

"Not so good," Abbie said, twisting her mouth and pursing her lips.

"Yes, not so good." Foster reached toward her, relieving her of the wilted flower she was still holding.

When he tossed it away and it fell softly to the ground, she gave a little sigh of disappointment, half expecting it to explode like a hand grenade or to emit a puff of smoke.

"Is the Queen bad? Or... evil?" Abbie looked up at Foster. "She sounds scary."

"Not evil," he replied. "Powerful. The Queens—there are two, of course—keep everything in our land running smoothly. They... well—of course, the stealing of children is bad, but that doesn't happen anymore." He looked sideways at her. "Not that I know of, anyway. And it isn't like the Queen herself is doing it."

Abbie frowned. "Sounds kind of evil to me."

"The Otherworld is tied to your world, and without the Queen's power to enforce the Bargains, both worlds would dissolve into chaos. Trust me. Also, the Queen of Summer is much, *much* better than the Winter Queen. Our Queen is light and fair and causes warmth and everything to grow, while the other Queen is as hard, cold, and unforgiving as her season."

"If your Queen is so nice then why are we running from her?" Abbie blew lightly on her skinned knee.

"She isn't nice; she is *fair*. Those who break rules are punished. And you do not wish to be punished, trust me."

"We should go. I still have something to show you." His green eyes twinkled as he changed the subject, and a smile lit up his sun-browned face. "Come!"

Abbie straightened her damp shorts and followed Foster as he worked his way between the trees.

"Isn't this like... a trail? Won't they follow us?" She looked behind them, worried.

"Keep watching," said Foster, stopping and waiting for a moment. Crumpled clover and bent branches stretched slowly back into place, erasing any visual proof of their path.

"Forest magic?" asked Abbie, her brown eyebrows raised high.

"Yes." Foster grinned at how much the small display had impressed her. "Elemental earth magic with a lean toward wood and plants." He put his hands on his hips, puffing out his chest with pride, and then beckoned for her to follow him again. "Come on. We should still hurry. The wolves can still catch our scent."

Not eager to meet the wolves, Abbie scrambled after Foster as he led her through the trees. Now that they were traveling at a normal pace, she could take time to see where the flowers grew in patches of sunlight and smell the rich earthiness of the forest. She ducked under a low branch and scrambled over a fallen log, the forest floor caking her feet in dirt. Nothing poked or pricked her feet, though—perhaps because of something magical Foster was doing, she considered.

The existence of magic was not that surprising to Abbie. Her parents had raised her on a steady diet of fairy tales (even the scary ones) and stories in which children fall through mirrors or wardrobes and end up in wondrous lands of enchantment and adventure. Her mother had always told her they were make believe, even if they were fun to think about, but her father had usually followed those statements with a wink.

Abbie liked to try to write her own stories, even if she didn't know how to spell all the words yet. Lately, all her writings had revolved around Sammy. He was an adventurous dog.

"Do the animals talk?" she blurted, hurrying to catch up with Foster and his longer legs.

He looked at her strangely. "Do they talk in your world?"

"Well, no. But I thought… maybe they do here. Sometimes in stories the animals talk. Like the wolves. Do they talk or just howl?"

"Oh," he said, holding a thin branch out of the way for her. "The animals are just like in your world. Mostly. Well," Foster paused, thinking. "There are animals here you will never see in your world. They talk to each other, but they do not talk like we do. The wolves are different, but it's hard to explain."

"Oh."

Abbie fell behind a step while she processed her disappointment. The trees thinned out, and she caught a whiff of something familiar in the air. Her stomach gurgled and growled, and she clutched it, suddenly remembering her lunch that she had been about to eat before the entire adventure had begun. The last she'd seen of it, it had been floating out in the middle of the pond.

The odor was unmistakable. "Bacon," she moaned, turning this way and that to try to see where the delectable smell was coming from. She followed her nose, wandering away from Foster before the boy realized what was happening.

Foster's carefully honed senses detected what they'd nearly walked into, and he lunged after her, his leaf shoes silent against the forest floor.

"*Stop*," he hissed, grabbing her arm just above the elbow and yanking her down behind a big leafy mass of raspberry canes. It was too late.

"Ow!" she cried, landing awkwardly on the ground. Foster grimaced at her, trying to communicate without talking, but she stuck her tongue out at him.

"What do we have here?"

Both youngsters looked up at the new voice. A dark-skinned woman with tightly cropped hair and a hawkish nose loomed over them from the other side of the raspberry thatch. She took a bite from a slice of bacon, and Abbie's eyes traced a long scar across the woman's right cheekbone that disappeared under her ear. It made for a scary visage as they looked up at her.

Foster scrambled to his feet, pretending that this was his plan all along.

"Merely picking berries," he said, standing as tall as he could.

The woman looked down at the thorny vines with their flowers and hard green fruits, and then back to the elf. He grit his teeth and touched the plant with a swirl of earth magic, ripening a handful of raspberries. He picked one and put it in his mouth, chewing without breaking eye contact with the stranger.

She grunted, amused, and finished off her bacon. Abbie watched every move of the tasty morsel until it disappeared.

"Nothing to do with that pack that was running a ways over, I imagine."

"Of course not," Foster said, expertly feigning offense. "I am an apprentice Guardian. Foster," he said, inclining his head just enough to be polite. The woman's eyes tracked to where Abbie was still sprawled on the ground, and the elf hurriedly helped the girl to her feet. "Just a… dryad," he said. "Newly born. I was showing her around the forest."

"Not very leafy for a dryad," mused the woman, her deep brown eyes shot through with gold.

Abbie kept her mouth shut, but her stomach growled, and Foster sagged, desperate to get her away.

"Ah, the birches are not known for being very, uh, leafy when they are new. Something you learn when you are a Guardian," he said, a bit too brightly, pulling Abbie close and slightly behind him.

"I'm sure it is," the stranger said. Then she smiled, her hardened face relaxing. "I am Nadiene. Come, join us." She gestured for Foster to walk around the berry thicket.

"Yes, please," said Abbie before she could stop herself.

"We should be going," Foster demurred simultaneously, meeting Abbie's eyes awkwardly.

She shrugged a little and grimaced. *Are dryads supposed to eat bacon? Well, this one is going to if she can get her hands on any.* Abbie inched along the raspberry canes, trying to make her way around without leaving her guide behind.

Foster squared his shoulders.

"We would be happy to accept your hospitality," he said formally, and the woman chuckled.

"Come on then, little ones." Nadiene stepped back from the raspberry vines while the human and elf made their way around to her campsite nestled in a grassy hollow. Lined on three sides by masses of thorny vines, it was a cozy little place with just enough room for her and her companion. "This is Charles," she said, taking a seat on the ground and leaning her elbow on a hummock of grass.

Charles was a thick-chested human with a fiery red beard, and he looked up with interest as the two children entered the camp. Both he and Nadiene wore weather-stained garments of sturdy cotton and leather, clothing made to stand up to the rigors of a life on the move. Foster's sharp eyes picked out the sheathed sword on the grass by Charles, and the long dagger belted to the woman's hip.

Abbie initially had eyes only for the tiny campfire and the cast iron pan resting on some stones beside it, but she slowed awkwardly at the presence of the hulking man. She was happy to slide behind Foster's more familiar presence as they approached the camp.

"Are you hungry?" Nadiene asked mildly, indicating the pan and the lonely bit of bacon lying limp inside it with a jerk of her chin.

Abbie looked at Foster questioningly.

"Dryads, of course, do not eat," he said tightly.

"No?" she said mournfully. "Maybe if I just... tasted it... to be sure?"

He turned toward her, staring at her fiercely when he thought the two adults couldn't see, and she sighed, sitting down on the grass.

"I would gladly share some bread," Foster said pointedly, even though he wasn't hungry. If formal hospitality rituals were observed, then he could relax.

Nadiene's scarred face stretched into another smile, and she dug into her bag. "I'm sure I had some here... Did you eat the bread, Charles?"

"No," he said. "We haven't had bread in days, since the last village."

"No bread, I'm afraid," she said to Foster, who pressed his lips together and looked back the way they'd come. "We need no bread or salt to extend the hospitality of our camp, such as it is, to you, young elf. And to your charge," Nadiene added, her eyes lingering on Abbie and her yellow T-shirt and denim shorts. "Be at ease—the wolves will not find you here."

"How did you know they were chasing us?" asked Abbie.

The adults shared a look while Foster groaned inwardly.

Nadiene leaned forward a little, speaking conspiratorially. "I understand the howls, little one. Please, eat the bacon before your stomach growls again. I know you are no dryad, no matter what our Guardian here says."

Not needing any more encouragement, Abbie scrambled over to where the pan sat, pulling the warm bacon free from the cooling grease. She let it drip for a second before eating it.

"You understand them because you *are* a wolf," said Foster with sudden understanding, a terrifying chill running through him. Face to face with danger instead of evading it as they'd so recently done, he found himself trying to decide whether to abandon Abbie and run for it, or stay by her side. He *was* responsible for her, to a certain extent. Sort of. Not *really*, though…

Foster shoved away his disloyal thoughts nearly as fast as he'd had them. No true Guardian of the Forest would abandon their task so quickly in the face of danger.

"Not one of the bootlickers," Nadiene said easily, the elf's wariness amusing her. "I have no master but myself."

Abbie licked her fingers clean, then frowned. "But you're a lady."

Charles laughed loudly at that, abruptly enough that both Foster and Abbie jumped, and so hard that tears formed in his eyes.

"She's no lady," he managed. Nadiene pitched her bag into Charles's belly, turning his laughter into wheezes for air.

"Your kind would call me a werewolf, I think," said the woman. "Here we are simply wolves."

"Not part of the Pack?" said Foster.

She had called them bootlickers, which had many interesting connotations, Foster considered. He gave the only exit from the hollow a sideways glance, gauging the distance.

"Not anymore," said Nadiene, leaning back once again. Her relaxed air now seemed like the languid posture of a predator, and the elf considered the Elements at his disposal.

Middling to no affinity for Air or Water. Moderate Fire. Excellent Earth with an emphasis on woodcraft, Foster thought. *Hiding is not especially useful when the enemy is already staring at you, but there is already a fire. It would not take much to—*

"*I* think you're good," said Abbie, interrupting Foster's escape plans. His mouth fell open at her abrupt proclamation.

"And why is that, little one?" asked the wolf, the corners of her mouth curling with amusement.

Abbie thought for a moment; she hadn't expected to have to back up her statement.

"The wolves chasing us are bad. Or, if they catch us, it'll be bad. And... you seem nice."

Faltering now, Abbie thought over everything her mom had ever told her about talking to strangers. She pushed herself up to her feet, reaching for Foster's hand.

"Perhaps I am only stalling you for the others," suggested Nadiene.

Charles grunted. "Now you're scaring them. Look, young elf, at my brand."

He pulled back the neck of his shirt, the laces loose enough to show a stylized rendition of the Tree of Life, the seal of the Summer Court, burned into the skin of his left breast. The old brand had a newer scar near it, a simple block rendering of an *F* hovering above the Tree. Both were long healed.

"Did that hurt?" asked Abbie, leaning forward.

"This one did," he rumbled quietly, touching the Tree. "The other I barely felt." His big finger traced the *F* under his collarbone. Charles looked at the elf, raising one eyebrow as Foster met his eyes. "Do you understand?"

"The brand means he was a slave in a Summer house—to a lord or lady of the Court," Foster said after a moment, explaining it to Abbie. "The letter above it indicates he was freed. He is human, like you, and is from your world."

The big, red-haired man covered the brands, meeting Nadiene's eyes before looking at the girl.

"The Queen will not take you, if I have anything to say about it."

"Thank you," Abbie said, uncertainly, still not quite sure what was going on. It had been a very busy afternoon. "Can you help me get back home? You... you could come, too. I mean, if you want."

"An excellent offer," Charles said kindly. "I am afraid we are not equipped to take on the Queen's guard, nor would I care to." He looked at Foster, who wasn't sure if he should be happy or sad that these adults seemed to be offering to take Abbie off his hands. "And you, elf, how came you to be in the company of a human child?"

"By accident," Foster muttered. He spoke up, "I found her in the woods by a pond." Abbie opened her mouth to expose his lie, and he amended quickly, "*In* a pond. I may have, ah, pulled her through."

A silence fell over the group. Nadiene said, after a moment, "You opened a gateway?" Charles shook his head with wonder, either at the accomplishment or at how stupid he'd been to do it—Foster couldn't tell which.

"I did not," he blurted, in case any nearby tree was listening. "I saw them open the Gate last Equinox, to let the Spring Boar through. It is a bit of Fire and Earth together . . . I was only playing at it. I did not think it would *work*."

"A fact I'm sure the Court will take into consideration," said the wolf woman dryly. "What are your names?"

"Abbie," said Abbie, smiling and trying to be polite.

"Foster," said the elf, sagging down into the grass.

"And you are a Guardian? Not quite yet, I think," mused Nadiene. "You're doing your trials, or soon will be, I wager, before the wood elves initiate you."

"Yes," admitted Foster, uncomfortable at how quickly he'd been laid bare.

He had much still to learn about guile, it seemed. His four-week sojourn into the Summer forests had just begun a few days ago. He could take nothing with him and had to find a suitable offering for the other Guardians to present to the Queen on his behalf. His parents had already bid him fare-well, for after this, if he was successful, he would live with the other Guardians, seeing his folks only on feast days. If he were not successful, like if he *accidentally* yanked a human girl through an unauthorized gate before being chased by wolves and forced into an unlikely partnership with a pair of obvious ne'er-do-wells, well, then all his hopes and dreams would be over, and his life might as well be over, too.

He looked down with surprise as Abbie scooted closer and put her smaller hand over his as it rested on the grass. She curled her fingers around his, finding comfort in the gesture. Even though she barely knew him, she *did* know him more than she knew the woman and the man.

"He's taking care of me," she said to the woman, trying hard not to stare at her scar.

Nadiene looked at the unlikely pair, and then to Charles, her partner. "There is *one* possibility."

Abbie perked up. "So, you *can* get me home?"

Charles looked at Nadiene blankly, and then straightened, his eyes sharpening as he shook his head. "That would be madness."

"What would be madness?" asked Foster, completely confused.

"Summer's Gate is too well guarded. But, there is another," the woman said, the gold in her brown eyes glittering in the sunlight.

"Oh no," said Foster, realization dawning.

"You're insane," said Charles, with respect in his voice. He grinned. "The Queen will not expect the girl to head for the border."

Nadiene smiled wolfishly. "As Summer waxes, Winter wanes. It would be your choice, of course, Abbie." She looked at the girl, who knit her brows together in thought.

She desperately wanted to go home. As amazing as her few hours in the Otherworld had been, she certainly didn't want to stay any longer than she had to. She missed her parents and Sammy, dreadfully. Abbie nodded, uncertainly, not sure what decision she was making. "I want to go home."

The werewolf sat back, satisfied. "Very well. We can take you to Winter's Heart."

CHAPTER 5

Reflections

THE SHADOWS STRETCHED across the hollow as the sun dipped toward night, and Abbie found herself time to think. Finding time to think was important, especially when you were far from home and surrounded by friendly strangers.

Charles was "getting dinner" with Foster, who had gone along just to keep an eye on the man after exacting binding promises from the woman that she would protect Abbie (and not trick her into any Bargains) while he was gone. She thought he was acting very stubbornly, considering how helpful the pair was being.

Abbie didn't really know what to think about Charles and Nadiene, so she tried to stay alert and on guard. Foster seemed not to trust them because Nadiene was a wolf, but she'd been nothing but nice to Abbie.

The girl glanced over at the self-proclaimed werewolf. Nadiene appeared to be sleeping.

Abbie put her face in her palms, squishing into a tight little ball as she sat, her knees pressed up against the back of her hands. What would her parents do in this situation? Obviously, her mother wouldn't have been wandering in the woods in the first place—when she had free time, she liked to curl up in the big cozy chair in the front room and read a book. Abbie sighed wistfully, picturing her mother with her nose in the latest novel, quietly turning pages until her phone rang, calling her away to another birth. When she had vacation time, they would go to a beach cottage and enjoy the coast, or cozy up in a log cabin in the mountains. Mom's time in the woods was always in the company of others.

Of course, Abbie knew what she was *supposed* to do if she ever got lost in the forest. Stay put. Guiltily, she remembered how she'd stormed away from the pond, trying to find her own way back home. *But,* she thought, *I couldn't go back the way I came, and Mom and Dad would never imagine looking through the bottom of a pond for me.* She could scarcely imagine it herself, and she'd been here for at least four whole hours.

A lazy butterfly fluttered over the raspberry vines behind her, landing on her right big toe. Abbie peeked through her knees, her cheeks smooshed up nearly into her eyes and her lips puckered between her hands. The butterfly was white, but as it moved through the last slivers of sunlight, a riot of pearly colors washed over the tiny fibers of its wings. The iridescent tones changed as it slowly opened and closed its wings, and she got the distinct feeling that it was showing off.

"Hi," she mumbled from her scrunched-up position, and the insect flew away. Abbie sighed.

Finding help to get home was great, but could she really trust any of these unfamiliar people? And if she couldn't, what was she supposed to do? Foster seemed to be the most trustworthy—he'd protected her from the Wee Folk and the wolves, and of course he'd opened a tree for them to hide in (*which was pretty much the best thing ever*, Abbie thought).

However, he didn't fully seem to trust these two adults they'd run into. Of course, he'd said, "I don't trust you," to Nadiene, so Abbie didn't need to be a genius to figure it out.

Charles seemed second best as far as Abbie's options for help went. He had nice eyes, even if his big red beard was a scraggly mess and his clothes were dirty. Her clothes were dirty, too, so you couldn't judge a person by that alone. He thought going to Winter was a bad idea, but he'd also grudgingly agreed that it was Abbie's best option if she didn't want to live in Otherworld forever.

Forever was a long, long time.

"Why are you going to help me?" she blurted, looking up at Nadiene.

The dark-skinned woman opened a golden eye. Perhaps she hadn't been asleep at all—or maybe she was a very light sleeper, like Abbie's dad.

"Maybe I like you," said Nadiene.

"Maybe," said Abbie, doubtfully. "But why?"

"We are between jobs. You need help." Nadiene glanced to the side as she talked, and Abbie considered what she said.

"What's your job?" She sat up a little straighter, her arms wrapping around her knees.

The wolf looked out past the raspberry vines to where her partner and the boy had disappeared, as if she could pull them back with sheer willpower. When she looked back to Abbie, the human girl was still sitting there, knees up, face turned toward her expectantly. She resisted the urge to sigh.

"We are thieftakers."

"You take… thieves?" Abbie screwed up her face in thought. "To the police?"

"Police?" Nadiene had to think about the word for a moment. "No, there are no 'police' here in Otherworld. The Pack—the other wolves—are most like your world's police, I suppose. But they do the bidding of the Queen and the high lords. Out here, in the villages of the Summer Fae, we take care of the ones who break the rules. For a price."

Abbie lapsed into silence once more, and the woman watched her cautiously, waiting for the next round of questions. From the look on the girl's face, it wouldn't be a long wait.

"But where do you take them? To the… Queen?"

"No, we round them up and take them to the—" she grimaced, pausing. "It's not really important."

Nadiene whisked past the details, Abbie's brown eyes watching her with intense and unnerving curiosity. "If you're a… bad guy, then a village might pay us to find you. And we would," she continued.

"What if the Queen pays you to find me?"

"She wouldn't."

"But what if she *did?*"

"She wouldn't," hurried Nadiene, before Abbie could open her mouth again, "But if she *did*, Charles would rather cut off his arm than hand you over. I don't think it would matter if she offered a vault of gold."

"He was like me."

"That he does—he likes you." The wolf smiled, and Abbie frowned.

"Not 'he likes me,' he *was like me*. A kid who ended up here. And he never went home."

Nadiene was trying to figure out a response to that when Foster and Charles returned to the hollow, a pair of rabbits in the big man's hand. Abbie's eyes widened at the sight of the dead animals, but she said nothing until Foster bounded over to her.

"Are you all right?" he demanded, looking suspiciously at Nadiene, who raised her hands in mute defense.

"Yeah, I'm okay," she said. Abbie looked sideways to where Charles was tossing the rabbits down on the grass, and then back to Foster. "Is that... dinner?"

She tried not to grimace, having been raised to be polite about what other people might offer to eat when she was at their home. Of course, this was not home, and she was not feeling particularly polite. She wrinkled her nose up as Charles sat down, getting ready to prepare the animals for dinner.

"Yes, the rabbits will suffice for a small meal," Foster said, but he misread her facial expression. "Do you have them in your world?"

"We have *bunnies*, yeah," Abbie said.

Charles pulled out a large knife and Abbie covered her face with her hands.

"They are already dead," Foster explained helpfully.

Abbie peeked through her fingers, her curiosity getting the best of her, and by the time Charles was cleaning the second rabbit, she had forgotten her fear.

Her stomach rumbled as Charles roasted the meat over the fire. "Won't the *wolves* smell them?" She whispered the word, as if naming them might bring the Pack down on their heads.

"The campsite is protected," said Nadiene, her first words since the others had returned. "Earth magic can be used for stealth or hiding. My talent is low but sufficient for a small area. Young Foster has bolstered the wards. We are safe for the night."

Foster blushed lightly as Abbie looked at him, the tips of his ears crimsoning. "I did not do that much," he mumbled, sitting down near her and watching the fire.

While the meat cooked, rendered fat sizzling into the fire from time to time, Abbie thought up a new line of questioning.

"Why did you warn me not to make any deals?"

"Because they are binding," Foster answered.

She narrowed her eyes slightly, and he continued. "It is different here than in your world. There is strong, ancient magic that seals agreements—such as deals and bargains—and makes them impossible to break. And if you somehow manage to break one, you will suffer."

Abbie screwed up her face as she considered that.

"Was it always like that?"

"Yes," said Foster, as Nadiene replied, "No."

Both children's heads swiveled toward the wolf. Their expectant and curious faces made her sigh, and she set aside her meal and cleared her throat.

"Thousands of years ago, before their ascensions, the Queens lived together. As close as sisters, for that is what they are, the two Fae women stood apart from the rest of the elves because of their effortless command of all the elemental magics.

"In those days, the Otherworld was full of wild magic, power generated by the land itself. Elves grew more powerful as they learned to harness wild magic, absorbing it and making it part of them. This is how some elves became the lords over others: their offspring inherited their great power.

"The sisters, each interested in different aspects of the elements, also sought out sources of wild magic, eventually separating and journeying across the Otherworld as their powers grew.

"During the Summer Queen's travels, she encountered an elf named Oberon. Oberon was powerful and handsome, and they became very close." Nadiene paused for a moment as Charles pulled the rabbits from the spit before continuing.

"Now, the Otherworld was wild, villages small and scattered, and the elves had not yet subjugated any of the other creatures. Oberon used his power to rule over a portion of the land, protecting many elves from the dangers around them. He was friendly with the wolves in his domain, and promises had passed between him and the Pack to never harm each other or those under his protection, and other such vows."

"Oh," interrupted Foster. "I think I have heard this story before."

"Well I haven't," said Abbie. She accepted a portion of meat from Charles without looking, her eyes locked on Nadiene. "What happened next?"

"The Alpha of the wolves had pledged his eldest daughter to the influential Oberon in marriage, to ensure the Pack's standing as equal beings to elves." Nadiene lifted a water skin and took a long drink. Wiping her mouth with the back of her hand, she said, "When the Summer Queen arrived and Oberon's attention was caught by her beauty, the Alpha bristled but thought the promise would still be upheld once the elven woman had gone on her way.

"However, Oberon was smitten by the Queen and she with him, and they soon decided to marry. Plans for a wedding were made and preparations took weeks, during which time the Alpha expected to hear from Oberon and grew more furious with each passing day.

"On the wedding day, the pledge between the Alpha and Oberon truly broken, the wolves swarmed into the elven castle and attacked those who had gathered to witness. In the battle, Oberon was grievously wounded. When the Pack finally withdrew, the Alpha made it clear to all that the elven lord had broken his vows to them, and this had been their retribution.

"Heartbroken, the Queen watched her love die, but not before Oberon expended his power to create a means to subjugate the wolves and ensure that no other elf fall prey to the Pack. After his death, and with this powerful object in hand, the Queen vowed that the tragedy of Oberon and his broken promises to the Alpha must never be repeated."

The fire crackled loudly, and Abbie jumped. Nadiene's eyes settled on her, glinting in the firelight.

"She returned home and met her sister once more, and together they bent their command of all the elements to spin a powerful spell, so that wherever one made a bargain or a deal, it would be sealed permanently. Weaker beings find themselves completely unable to contradict the Bargains made, and those who are strong and might break one wither and die shortly after.

"After a time, the sisters used this spell to create the Accords, the binding agreements that created and keep the balance between the Seasons and the Otherworld's relationship with your world, Abbie."

Nadiene fell silent.

"So you can't break a promise here? At all?" Abbie glanced at Charles, thinking of his pledge to keep her safe.

"You have to use specific language. 'A bargain is struck,' or something to that effect," rumbled Charles. "You can feel the magic taking effect when you do."

Later, when they'd finished dinner and stoked the fire, Abbie wrapped a musty blanket they'd given her around her shoulders, snuggling up as best she could on the ground. The stars had come out. She thought of the many clear evenings she'd spent with her father in the backyard, lying in the grass staring up at the night sky. She'd become passably familiar with the constellations and planets that filled their galaxy.

Thinking about her dad made her chin quiver. Her eyes filled with tears, and she blinked hard, trying to pick out the Big Dipper. The more she looked, the more stars she could see. Hundreds, thousands of stars, and suddenly a big milky swirl of them stretched over her in an arc, but she couldn't see anything that looked familiar.

Turning over, she stared with bleary eyes into the coals of the fire. She would go home. She would see her dad and mom again, she told herself. Even if she had to trust some people she normally wouldn't, or do things she'd never done before—she would do it. Abbie squeezed her eyes shut as the tears came and buried her face into the borrowed blanket that smelled like old leather, crying silently until she fell into an exhausted sleep.

Breakfast consisted of some hard biscuits Nadiene had in her bag and leftover rabbit from the night before. The meat was cold and gamey, but Abbie ate it without complaint. The morning air was cool; the blanket enveloping her barely kept the goosebumps at bay.

If she was going to travel into the other realm of the Fae, into the heart of Winter as Nadiene had said, she might freeze to death before she could get there.

"I'm gonna need some more clothes," she said abruptly. "And shoes." She looked at Foster and his leaf shirt and short pants, shaking her head. "You, too."

"What?" Foster looked down at himself. "I am fine."

"Not for snow," said Abbie.

"I do not go into the snow," said Foster. "I am a summer elf."

"But that's where I'm going." She looked at him with hesitation. "Aren't you... you're coming with us, right?"

"I... ah, that is..." the young elf looked at the wolf and the human man, but Nadiene was busy packing her bag and Charles was content to simply watch the two children talk. "Surely you do not need me to come with you into Winter."

Foster's heart raced simply considering it. How would his warm summer magic fare in Winter? And the other Guardians, they were waiting for him to complete his quest.

Abbie's lower lip trembled. "But you're *responsible* for me."

He took in a deep breath and exhaled slowly. "I have to finish my trial. Lady Nadiene and Sir Charles," he began, unsure why he was conflating their titles, "have graciously offered you companionship to Winter's Gate where you might slip through unnoticed. The summer equinox draws near, after all. It's the time of greatest weakness for the Winter elves."

Charles grunted. "Sounds like you know a lot about Winter elves."

"Yes—wait, no! No, I do not know that much," Foster quickly tried to backtrack, but it was too late.

"We could use someone who knows what we're getting into. I mean, we know, but we don't *know* like an elf knows."

Abbie frowned, trying to parse the sentence, but it sounded like Charles was on her side when it came to getting Foster to come along. She smiled hopefully, looking at the elf boy.

"You can help! *Pleeeeease?*"

"The height of Summer may be the weakest time for Winter, but the border will still be closely monitored by wards and wolves. I can help with the latter—we will need your help with the former," Nadiene declared. She looked up from her bag. "Come with us to the border, at least."

"I... suppose that would be all right," said Foster, but an uneasy feeling swelled in his stomach as he agreed.

"Who knows, you may find a prize worthy of the Queen on the journey," Nadiene said with a wink, but the light in her brown and gold eyes was unsettling.

"Then it's settled," boomed Charles, making Abbie jump. He laughed. "We should be moving on." He looked at Abbie's bare feet. "There is a village not too far from here. We can get you boots there."

"Not without exposing her," snapped Nadiene, frowning.

"I have an idea," smiled Charles.

CHAPTER 6

Touch and Go

"SHE'S SICK," FRETTED Fiona, checking Abbie's temperature once more. Dan stood in the doorway of his daughter's room, his arms at his side while he watched his wife read the digital thermometer. "A hundred and four." She pressed her palm to her daughter's feverish forehead as Abbie sat patiently on the edge of her bed.

"I'm okay, Mommy," said Abbie, smiling with bravery.

Abbie looked pale, and maybe even a little thinner since the night before.

"You're going to be fine," Fiona promised, giving her a kiss on her hairline. "Lie down, okay? You need your rest. I'll be back in a minute with some Tylenol for you."

Abbie obediently snuggled down into her comforter, hugging her stuffed bear she'd called "Big-Eyed Teddy" since she was four.

"Should I take her to Doctor Tom?" asked Dan as his wife passed him in the doorway. "Just to be sure?"

Fiona pursed her lips, pausing in her quest for medicine.

"It's just a fever for now. I don't think we need to call the pediatrician yet—but if it doesn't go down, or if she gets another symptom, then yeah, I'll talk to him."

She leaned forward and pecked him on the cheek before disappearing into their shared bedroom.

Dan leaned back into Abbie's room, looking at the little girl on the bed. Her brown hair clung damply to her face, and she opened her eyes, making eye contact with him. "Daddy," she called softly, holding her hand out toward him. After a moment's hesitation, he went to her side.

"What is it?"

He swept her lovingly crocheted baby blanket over her, tucking her outstretched arm in close to her body. Big-Eyed Teddy stared at him reproachfully from under her chin.

"I feel strange." She wiggled under the blanket, freeing her arms and plucking at his shirt. "I need a hug."

Abbie's eyes filled with water, as if she were about to cry, and then Fiona bustled in with the Tylenol in a little cup, brushing Dan aside.

"Here you go, sweetie."

Fiona tucked the girl's hair behind her ears and helped her sit up to drink the medicine. Abbie dutifully drank the purple liquid, and then threw her arms around her mother in a tight hug.

"I wish you didn't have to go to work," she said, her face pressed against Fiona's shirt. "Can't you stay with me?"

Fiona looked up at Dan, grimacing as their daughter's pleas broke her heart.

"You know I have to go to work. Daddy will be here, like always. Everything will be fine. Just rest, okay, honey?"

"Okaaaay," said Abbie, drawing out the word as she clung to Fiona.

Dan wanted to leap forward to separate them, but he couldn't—not without tipping his hand or horrifying his wife. He forced a smile as Fiona extricated herself from Abbie's arms, promising she'd be back as soon as she could. No births today—not that there couldn't be a surprise—just office visits.

"I'm going to be late."

She kissed Abbie's warm forehead and stood, blowing another kiss through the air as she backed toward the door to make her escape from the bedroom.

Dan smiled at the girl in the bed. "Get your rest. Do you want a book to read?"

"No, thank you," said Abbie. She wiggled down into her blankets and closed her eyes. He left the room, closing the door quietly behind him, and caught up to Fiona before she ran out the front door.

She caught his expression and paused.

"What's worrying you?" Then she looked at her phone, her eyes widening at the time. "It's going to be okay. Call me later?"

"Sure."

Dan kissed her goodbye before she hurried out the door to her car. He walked down the hall toward the kitchen, mulling over the recent events in his mind. He needed to talk to someone about his thoughts, someone familiar with the Otherworld.

"How did you get this number?"

"Does it matter?" he replied.

Dan sat on the kitchen counter, tethered to the wall by the phone. It was strange to be talking to Mathan, so many years after the Great Hunt had been disbanded. The great werebear had been one of his trusted lieutenants before... *before we were scapegoated by the Queens and thrown into permanent exile.*

He couldn't help but frown at the thought, creasing his brow in regret.

A sigh. "Was a time you could call me up and I would follow you through hell, Wodan. That was a long time ago."

"I know. Things have changed since the Hunt—"

"The Hunt no longer exists," Mathan said flatly. "The Gates were closed behind us when we came through, and the Boar runs wild in the worlds. And it's not my problem, whatever it is. Don't call me again."

"There's been an incursion. A changeling."

The silence on the line lasted for so long, Dan wondered if Mathan had hung up already. Then, "How do you know?"

"It's my daughter."

Another pause, and then a weary sigh. "Killing it is—"

"I can't do that. Not yet, anyway." Dan frowned deeper. "Its existence is a violation of the truce."

"Not much we can do about it from this side of the Gates."

"You know as well as I do that it can't be the first intrusion since the Queens signed the Accords. Summer is making a move."

"And if you keep the changeling around, one of them will have a powerful agent to do her bidding."

They both knew that changelings could access magic with impunity in the human world. The entire reason the Gates had been sealed was to keep the balance between Summer and Winter and stop the incessant power plays from taking over the world. That Wodan and the Great Hunt had been selected as the joint sacrifice after he had turned down Titania's invitations to join her court was not likely a coincidence. It was, however, a truth he had kept from the others of the Hunt.

"Well, one of them has decided the risk is worth it. Probably Summer."

"Titania is too smart for that."

"Too smart to get caught. The Gates are sealed. If Winter holds to the Accords, they will never find out until it's too late."

"Global warming," Mathan said suddenly. "I wondered if perhaps Summer was growing in power, but if this is true—if they sent the changeling…" His deep voice trailed away.

Dan picked up where Mathan left off. "It's a long game she's playing. One that could change this world forever."

"She cares nothing for the human world, you know that. The elven lords of her court will follow her whims and fight over the scraps of what's left."

"Bold words, even for a bear," Dan said, cracking a smile that quickly faded as he thought of the call he'd had made the night before. "I contacted the Cat."

Mathan sucked in his breath in a hiss. "The Cat cares about nothing but herself."

"She has access to the Otherworld," Dan pointed out. "She has her magic, even here in the human world. Even though she's a dragon, she's as close to a neutral party between Seasons as exists in the worlds."

"The dragons are too capricious to trust. Neutral or chaotic. Who can tell what they get out of their deals until it's too late?" Dan remained silent for a few moments, and Mathan continued. "Better to kill it and move on. The girl is beyond your reach, even if she still lives."

The pragmatic words rankled, and Dan took a breath to calm the surge of anger welling inside him. Once before, he would have trusted and acted upon the advice his old friend gave him. Who could predict the whims of Queens, other than understanding their apparent predilection toward screwing his life up? Dan rubbed a spot between his eyes, closing them briefly.

"Daddy?"

He looked up, startled. "Why are you out of bed?"

Abbie stood by the kitchen table a few feet away, darkening circles under her eyes.

"I don't feel so good."

"I know. Just go back upstairs to rest, please."

Mathan sighed on the other end of the open line.

"Don't call this number again, Wodan. I have made the best of this life… and I cannot help you."

There was a click, and the phone went silent in his hand. Dan's face hardened, and his hand tightened on the receiver until his knuckles whitened. Instead of yanking the phone from the wall and throwing it against the refrigerator door, he carefully hung it up and turned toward the changeling child.

"I thought you were asleep."

He could see the girl (who looked so much like Abbie it made his heart ache) making those small movements that meant she was preparing to run at him. Not to hurt him, not exactly anyway, but to hug him. He had been minimizing his contact with her since he'd realized what she was, trying to keep the changeling at bay without alarming his wife, and he was still trying to decide how best to handle the creature. Murder it, and he would lose Fiona and his carefully crafted life. But live in denial about the girl, and he would lose his real daughter and possibly everything else in the end anyway.

Abbie darted at him, and he caught her before she wrapped her arms around him, holding her at arm's length. Her big brown eyes welled up with tears, and she grabbed at his forearms.

"Let me stay up with you. I'm sad," she moaned.

"Why are you sad?"

Dan gently pushed her away, but she came back at him in the way children do: octopus-like in the way they could latch on to a caregiver's limbs. He kept shifting his hands but couldn't bring himself to shut her down completely, and she took advantage, slipping inside his reach at last and snuggling against his side. Her little body was hot with fever, and his heart ached at how much she looked like his girl.

"I'm lonely up there." Abbie looked up at him as he reluctantly put his arm around her. "Can we watch TV?"

An automatic refusal was on the tip of his tongue, but he nodded in spite of himself.

"A little TV sounds like a good idea. Meet me on the couch?"

Abbie's face brightened despite her illness, and she hurried off into the living room. Dan followed more slowly, gathering a big blanket from a closet, and setting her up with a snuggle-nest on the couch before he took his seat beside her, but not too close.

Sammy watched reproachfully from the other side of the room but wouldn't come any closer. Since his return to the house, the dog had given the child a wide berth, scrambling to avoid getting close to her. Dan couldn't blame the little dog—he knew he sensed the difference—and the changeling showed no interest in him at all, which Fiona chalked up to her illness. Normally patient with how the terrier only listened to her husband and daughter, Fiona had become noticeably frustrated with Sammy's uncharacteristic behavior.

From what Dan knew, changelings were creatures of almost pure magic and needed nourishment to grow into their full strength. If they were denied love and affection, they would wither and die. In fact, when the Queens actively fought so many years ago, they sent many changelings into the world to battle for supremacy on their behalf. The devastated parents of the replaced children would often leave the changelings out to die, in the hopes that their own child would be returned to them. They were not, of course, but the agents of the Seasons were thwarted by the cold-hearted treatment, often withering away and dying in the woods.

The humans have written this into their histories as ignorant superstition, perhaps paving the way for…whatever this is, here and now, Dan mused.

Just bad luck, then, that I am the one who… but am I the only one?

Dan glanced down at the child near him, feverish eyes staring dully at the cartoon animals cavorting about on the screen and wondered again if perhaps Summer had been sending the creatures for years. And, even if Titania had been, was that so bad? Summer striking a blow and winning the war of the Seasons once and for all could be good for him.

Perhaps he could finally go home.

Dan looked down at Abbie, the changeling, remembering the day his daughter had been born. Taking a wife as successful as Fiona had been calculated, but she had convinced him they should start a family together. That was over eight years ago, and he had acquiesced to keep her happy. He had always felt affection toward Fiona, but when the human doctor had placed their baby girl into his arms and he looked into Abbie's eyes for the first time while his wife lay sweaty and accomplished on the birthing bed, he had been changed forever. Love had bloomed toward the tiny person he held and taken a firm root in his heart.

With as much dedication as he had ever put toward driving the Great Hunt forward, Dan had thrown himself into fatherhood. It seemed that Titania was destined for the last laugh, however, her plans managing to toss his life into disarray once again.

The child coughed, ending with a little painful moan that sounded so much like Abbie that Dan wanted to gather her into his arms. He steeled himself against the impulse. They stared at the television as a pair, she with one hand sticking out of the blankets for him to take, and he with his arms crossed, jaw set.

CHAPTER 7

Journey Through Summer

FOSTER WALKED BESIDE Charles into the elven village of Berryhaven, the artificial bounce in his step disguising the ill ease he felt in his heart. The rules of his trial *specifically* stated that he must stay apart from elven habitations. Habitations and villages *exactly* like the one he was journeying into. The floppy hat that hid his curls did nothing to keep him from erupting in nervous sweat.

No one will find out," Charles had said, back at the camp, an hour before.

It will be fine. But the girl is right: you need better clothes," Nadiene had said.

She'd surveyed his clothing with a critical eye. Foster wrinkled his nose and grimaced at her leathers while fingering his leafen shirt. Spun from magic, the fabric of his shirt could change colors to match the surrounding plants. It was a fine thing to wear… in the realm of Summer.

"Then you do it!" Foster protested to the thieftakers.

"A man my size, buying children's clothes?" Charles shook his head. "I am well known in the area, and they know I have no family. It will raise more questions than we wish to answer. An elf boy trading for clothes for himself? Perfectly acceptable."

"She can wear the same size as you," added the wolf. "It will add more warmth, anyway."

Abbie, the cause of all this nonsense and frippery, had looked up at Foster with those trusting brown eyes, and he felt an intense stab of guilt in his guts. *For is it not* my *fault, after all, that she is even here?*

"I'll do it," he'd grumbled between gritted teeth.

Here he was, stepping into the nearest village in search of furs and sturdy clothing. Cold weather clothes were not a thing one could just go to the mercantile and buy, of course, for there was no need for warm clothing in Summer; however, Charles had said he could stitch together something warm enough for the children to wear on the journey, if given the right materials.

Nadiene, Charles, and Abbie watched Foster disappear past the first row of cottages down the main street of Berryhaven from the tree line.

"What if the wolves come back?" asked Abbie.

"They won't," said Nadiene flatly.

"But what if they *do?*"

"I will put you on my shoulders while I fight them off." Charles winked, and Abbie relaxed with a grin.

There was something about the big man that reminded her of her father, though they couldn't look more different. Both were tall, but Charles was broad, thick, and ruddy while Dan was slim and pale with fine features. Charles's fiery beard nearly covered his mouth entirely, but he was quick to laugh, winked at her when he caught her looking, and she felt safe around him.

Nadiene narrowed her eyes when the girl glanced at her with another question on her lips, and Abbie fought the urge to stick her tongue out. Her father always encouraged her to ask questions. "It's how we learn," he had said.

"Now what?" asked Abbie.

"Now we wait," said the thieftaker, taking a few steps back into the trees. "Quietly."

Abbie did stick out her tongue and cross her eyes behind Nadiene's back, and Charles caught her. He winked. She grinned, blushing.

The opposite side of the village had a few acres of fields, but Berryhaven was a small hamlet, dependent on commerce with larger towns. There was little traffic this time of day, but the trio stayed hidden from the main road leading toward Mapleton, a bigger town close in trade with the elves of Berryhaven.

The girl felt intensely curious about the elves and how they lived. From everything she'd read, she had expected the town to be completely made of treehouses, or spun out of gleaming glass on the side of a mountain, or something more than just picturesque rows of stone cottages.

"How long is it going to take?" she asked.

"Not long," said Nadiene curtly.

"Be nice," said Charles, shouldering his pack. Abbie looked up from where she sat, startled, and he smiled to reassure her. "I'm going to town, too, for supplies. Fear not, the fair maiden will guard you," he said, gesturing toward the scar-faced wolf. "I will keep an eye out for young Foster."

"Okay," she said in a small voice, and then Charles's comforting presence was gone, leaving her with Nadiene and her stern silences.

"Ahoy, the camp!" A small, familiar voice bubbled from a nearby tree.

Abbie scrambled to her feet, looking around wildly. Nadiene remained lounging against an oak, but her golden eyes were sharp, picking out the tiny figures surrounding them in the trees.

"Table?" breathed Abbie, her heart thumping at the sight of the fairy and his applewood twig.

He had acquired an acorn cap helmet since the day before, and it sat rakishly on his head.

"The one and same," intoned the fairy, sketching out a bow in midair as other fairies flitted in and out of the surrounding trees. "Do you want to play?"

"She does not," Nadiene interrupted, sending a quick shiver down Abbie's spine.

"Yeah," said Abbie slowly, and Table perked until she continued. "No playing. I don't like playing."

"I sense a lie in you," said the tiny man, his eyes narrowing. "Yet, we will be on our way," he added hastily as Nadiene shifted her position on the ground. "With just one question more. Have you an idea where the Thimble may be?"

"The what?" growled Nadiene, her right hand visibly inside her pack as she glared at the fluttering fairies.

"A powerful talisman that can break any spell!" tittered Fork (or was it Rug?), the tiny winged woman alighting upon Abbie's shoulder. The girl started but stood as still as she could while the fairy pushed her long brown hair over her ear, the strands thick like yarn in Fork's hands. "Oh, there you are," giggled the fairy, peering toward Abbie's eye as she kept her balance with two fistfuls of hair. "What *lovely* ears," Fork continued, her tiny hands grabbing hold of the edges of Abbie's ear as she leaned in and bellowed a *"HULLO"* down into it.

Abbie yelped, and Fork flew off, laughing as the girl clapped her hand over her ear.

"Stop it!" She waved her free hand in the air to keep the fairies out of her face, catching one of the Wee Folk off guard. Unexpectedly batted out of the air, he spiraled to the ground. Abbie gasped apologetically as the fairy flopped about on the moss.

Table swooped down, crying, "First blood!"

As he inspected his fallen friend, Abbie observed them, gently kneeling to the ground. The fairy seemed dazed rather than hurt as Table pumped his limbs up and down, testing functionality. The fairy fluttered his wings experimentally.

"He's not bleeding," Abbie retorted as Table glared at her over his shoulder.

"A close call," the fairy allowed. He picked up his twig and shouldered it, standing with a fist on his hip as he stared up at Nadiene and Abbie. He settled his gaze on Nadiene, boldly turning his back on the girl. "The Thimble. We must find it."

"Is it yours?" asked the wolf, still reclining against a tree trunk. Her golden eyes flicked past the fairy to where Abbie stood and then returned to Table's miniature face.

"It belongs to us!" He jerked the stick from his shoulder and pointed it at her in a blink. "You will tell me where it is!"

"Be calm," Nadiene muttered. "I do not have a thimble, important or otherwise. I am a wolf and a thieftaker; I have no need for enchanted items, nor the tools for sewing." She sighed and cast her gaze back toward the hamlet.

Table spun, pointing his wooden staff at Abbie next, who flinched despite herself.

"Perhaps she will tell me what you will not."

"Leave the girl alone, or I'll not play nice." The wolf's eyes were flat and hard.

The leader of the Wee Folk lit up as if Nadiene had turned on a lightbulb, and he shot into the air. Abbie could imagine a trail of pixie dust trailing off him as he cavorted.

"Play nice! Yes! We shall play!"

Nadiene grimaced in understanding, as the forest suddenly burst alive with Wee Folk. They swarmed through the small clearing, and Abbie darted to Nadiene's side. She huddled there as Table lighted upon Nadiene's knee, his face aglow with delight.

"What game shall we play?" He put his hand on his chin and looked up, thoughtfully. "Rhymes? Riddles? Feats of strength?" He looked slyly at the wolf woman as he said the last part wagging a finger at her. "Perhaps not."

Nadiene hesitated before answering. A small group of fairies could quickly grow into an unruly swarm if games were afoot. Her only choice was to finish the game as quickly as she could.

"Rhymes." Nadiene forced a smile. "May I go first?"

"No!" Table flew off, hovering out of arm's reach. The rest of the Wee Folk settled into the neighboring trees, the air suddenly quiet except for the whirring of Table's wings. "Ahem." He pulled at his shirt, adjusting it, and turned a figure eight in the air.

"To begin this game, one must always explain the rules to those who don't know how it goes. A rhyming verse, this is how you'll curse your opponent to finish what you've beginnish."

Abbie frowned, opening her mouth, but Nadiene clapped her hand over the girls' face, muffling her. The fairy continued.

"So this I'll start, my rhyme comes from the heart. Tell me of the Thimble…"

Nadiene thought for a moment while Table buzzed back and forth, then began, continuing the verse Table had left unfinished. "And make your words nimble. I know little of grand searches, though you may check by the birches, or by trees with leaves of orange…"

Table squinted, thinking. "But to do so takes courage. The quest will take all your might, to face down your—"

"That doesn't rhyme!" blurted Abbie. "Orange and courage?"

Table pulled up short, flustered. "Of course it does."

"Beginnish isn't a word, either," she added.

"It is. I said it, so it is a word."

The leader of this band of Wee Folk whipped his head to look around at his people clustered in the trees, watching and whispering to each other.

"You have lost, Table," said Nadiene. "Give over."

He stamped his foot in midair, his small face a thundercloud.

"Fine! You win this time, wolf. Next time we play it will be *riddles*." He waved his stick, and the Wee Folk erupted from the branches, filling the air. Table paused. "Did you really hear it is by leaves of orange?"

The wolf snarled, and he zipped back a foot or so.

"You have defeated me, and we will leave, as is proper. No need for that. Good day."

He gave them a half-hearted bow, and then the cloud of Wee Folk departed through the trees.

Abbie slumped against Nadiene's side. "Wow."

"A small annoyance," the woman said. "But they have a taste for games and mischief, and may be back." Nadiene took Abbie's face in her hands, studying her. "It is good your hair is long. Covers your ears, mostly, anyway."

She arranged the girl's hair so it framed her face.

"What's wrong with my ears?" asked Abbie, suddenly self-conscious. The dark-skinned woman gave Abbie a look, and it dawned on her. "Ohhh, because they're normal. Or, not normal, I guess."

She tugged on her brown hair, holding it tightly against her head.

"The Queen still searches for you. The fewer people who see a young human girl in the woods, the better."

Nadiene scratched her scalp through her own close-cropped hair.

"Do you think Table will tell on me?"

"If put to the question, he certainly will. But," Nadiene added quickly, "It is difficult to catch the Wee Folk. What they lack in size they make up for in speed and numbers. They are not anyone's first choice when it comes to finding information."

"What if they go tell the Queen?" Abbie worried.

"It is not likely that they will do so," Nadiene said. "In any case, we will not be here long, and they don't know where we might be heading."

She awkwardly patted Abbie's head. "Best not to worry about it."

They were still sitting there when Foster arrived with a paper-wrapped bundle under his arm and a pile of furs draped over one shoulder.

"How'd it go?" asked Abbie.

"It… went well." Foster flopped cross-legged onto the ground and passed the package to Nadiene. Abbie crouched near him, and he handed her one of the furs. "Rabbit," he said, and she marveled at how soft it was.

"Why didn't we just use the skins from last night's dinner?" she asked.

"The hide has to be tanned and treated," answered Nadiene, turning the fur over in the girl's hand to reveal the underside. "It's a process that takes time."

"Oh, right."

Abbie sat quietly, petting the fur and wondering about the little animal that had worn it. It made her sad to think about, but the fur was also something she needed to keep warm if they were traveling into Winter. Nadiene passed her a pair of brown pants, a tooled leather belt, and a cream-colored tunic. Abbie handed back the fur while she went to change behind one of the bigger trees.

When she returned, she gave a little spin to show off the slightly oversized clothes, and the wolf nodded her approval.

"Good. You will not stand out so much now."

The package held another set of clothing for Foster and a pair of light wool cloaks.

Foster dropped a pair of soft boots by Abbie's dirty, bare feet, and she grinned.

"Oh! Thank you!"

Abbie washed her feet from a canteen of water, wiggling her toes with satisfaction when they were finally clean and dry and wrapped up in socks and boots.

"I guessed at your size," said Foster, watching the whole shoe-putting-on ceremony with fascination.

"They're perfect," she said, beaming. She hugged him impulsively before he realized what she was doing. "Thank you!"

"What did I miss?" boomed Charles, startling Abbie as he rejoined them. "Ah, you look a proper village elf now," he said, ruffling her hair. "Well done, Foster."

"Thank you," the boy muttered self-consciously.

"The Wee Folk came back," blurted Abbie, and Nadiene nodded when the others looked to her for confirmation.

"They are on some ridiculous quest for sewing supplies," the wolf said. "Luckily for us, they never remember that nothing rhymes with orange."

"Could they actually hurt us?" asked Abbie. "They're just so small and funny." She gave another experimental twirl in her new outfit and boots.

"They could—they are capricious creatures, but also easily distracted or defeated as long as you can keep your wits about you. The best defense is not to engage, but if they force you into a game, try to choose rhymes and remember *orange*," winked Nadiene. "If you use it on the same Wee Folk clan too many times, however, they get quite cross. Their ability with magic is larger than their size indicates. They can turn the forest against you. I knew a wolf who ate a few fairies when they angered him, and the rest of the clan cursed all his hair from his body and then set the trees against him. He was lost in the woods for weeks, and he was never quite the same afterward."

Abbie nodded seriously, her eyes widening as she imagined a hairless wolf. She sat on a mossy root while the adults divided up the food Charles had bought into their packs. They placed a portion of the food inside a small bag for Abbie to carry, along with her own flint.

"I will show you how to use it tonight," said Charles.

"No, I know how," she said. "My dad and I go camping, and he taught me."

A lump rose in her throat and tears pricked her eyelids as she wondered if she would ever see her parents again. Abbie looked away from Charles to her little pack, swallowing hard.

Charles put a comforting hand on Abbie's shoulder, just for a moment, and she straightened, looking up with determination through eyes shining with unshed tears.

"A practical man," said Charles softly. "Then you shall start the fire tonight."

He helped Abbie put her pack on her shoulders, and she wiggled a bit to make sure it was comfortable. Foster procured his own bag and slung it across his back while the wolf stood and gave herself a shake.

Then they were off, putting Berryhaven to their backs and weaving their way through the forest toward the border of the Seasons.

CHAPTER 8

Dragon's Den

"I'M TAKING HER to Doctor Tom."

Dan stroked groggily for the shores of his dream as Fiona's voice filtered into his subconscious, then, as understanding washed over him, he awoke abruptly.

"Is it that bad?" He searched his wife's concerned face, half aware that he'd slept in his clothes after finally passing out the night before.

"It's more than just a summer cold," she answered, the space between her eyebrows deepening into a pair of worry lines. "Not eating, fevers, vomiting... she's wasting away, Dan."

He opened his arms, and she sat beside him on the bed, letting him fold her into a hug. Fiona sighed against his neck, her body relaxing only slightly.

"If you say she needs to go, then we'll take her." Dan kissed her forehead and frowned. "You feel warm, too."

"I've been running around." Fiona pushed back a little and kissed his cheek. "She doesn't even want anything to do with Sammy—actually I can't get him to go near her, either."

She made a frustrated noise. "Usually I'm trying to keep him out of her bed at night, but he's been sleeping under the table in the dining room."

Fiona looked down at her husband's rumpled clothes with a raised eyebrow, as if to say, *speaking of people with strange sleeping habits of late…*

"It's probably nothing." He put his hand on her forehead. "Are you sure you're all right?"

"I'll worry about myself when she's better," said Fiona. "I've asked Dr. Stevens to cover my patients for the next week. I feel like this is a sign that I need to spend more time with her. And you, too," she added, rubbing her nose on Dan's before untangling herself and getting up. "I got her an early appointment, so I need to get her dressed and ready."

"Of course." Dan followed her out of the bed, stopping and stretching to work out the kinks of a restless night. "Do you want me to come?"

"I can handle it." Fiona snagged her shoes from under the bed. "Someone called for you this morning around four; I didn't want to wake you up. Can you tell them not to call so early—or late—next time?"

"Who was it?"

"Someone named Cat. She said…" Fiona paused and thought for a moment. "I wrote it down so I wouldn't have to remember," she sighed, "but something about a meeting downtown today."

"Huh," he said, doing his best impression of nonchalance while his wife studied him curiously. "She's an old colleague. But if you and Abbie," he nearly choked on the name, "need me…?"

"If you need a little me-time to catch up with old friends, you should take it. I have the time off work, so you should keep the meeting." Fiona finished tying her shoes. "I'll let you know how it goes with Doctor Tom. And you should shower before you try visiting with old work friends."

Dan gave his wrinkled T-shirt a concerned sniff. "Eau de sick child?"

"Eau de Pepé le Pew," Fiona teased. She kissed him good-bye. "See you later."

"Tell... Abbie she's going to be fine," he replied. *And you are going to be fine*, he thought, focusing on his love for his true daughter. *I will find you and bring you home again.*

The Cat sat sideways in her chair as Dan approached, her legs crossed and toes artfully pointed. A pair of lime green heels lay haphazardly on the polished wood floor where she'd let them fall.

"I have to say, I did *not* expect to hear from *you*." Her voice was a throaty purr, and she tossed her long purple hair over her tattooed shoulder as she sat up. The brick walls and exposed ductwork in the building seemed industrial downstairs, but the Cat's loft was hipster chic.

Very quiet, too. Dan could barely hear the traffic outside.

"You know why I'm here."

He stood firm a few feet away from her chair. One could describe the piece of furniture the Cat reclined upon as a throne, but he didn't want to give her the satisfaction, even in his thoughts. The rest of the room was bare, except for some abstract art hung on the brick.

Dan forced himself to make eye contact with the creature, for the Cat was not a human woman, but an ancient shape-shifter. She was, in fact, one of the few surviving dragons from the Otherworld, even if her treasured hoard was information and not gold.

Although, it was probably gold, too.

"Indeed, I do. My secretary is quite good," the Cat said, her amber eyes with their odd, vertical pupils focusing on him. She smiled suddenly. "You should see your face, Wodan. Imagine, *you*, so worried about a mere child. I never thought I'd see the day when you cared about something more than yourself, let alone the day when something existed that the Hunter could not find."

She lifted a manicured hand, and a file folder floated off a side table toward her. Plucking it from the air, the Cat flipped it open.

"And a wife, too." She made a noise in her throat that Dan realized was a chuckle. "To risk your exile by exposing," she expelled a rancid laugh again, "yourself like this—your time here in the world has changed you more than I thought possible."

"I'm not here to talk about me." Dan crossed his arms over his chest and widened his stance. "I want to know what you've heard about my daughter."

"No need to be rude," the Cat said sharply. "You are the one here for a favor. It costs you nothing to indulge me, and yet you want to push past all the fun."

He raised an eyebrow as his heart beat faster, considering the Cat's chosen name. She was a powerful creature, especially here where her kind were among the few who could touch the magic of the Otherworld. She was also used to getting her way.

"Cats tend to play with their food. Forgive me if I refuse to be toyed with."

"Wonderful creatures, aren't they?" the Cat mused, ignoring the latter part of his comment.

"A little smaller than a dragon," he said, staring at her, and she laughed.

"One makes their allowances to live among the humans. You have hidden your ears, and apparently your spine, while

I…" the Cat gestured down at her slim, feminine body. "Your girl is not the first to find herself in the Otherworld, and she won't be the last. I don't do house calls anymore. Too messy. So, if you want her out, you're going to have to get her yourself."

He clung to hope. "So she's alive?"

The Cat smiled, an ugly expression on her beautiful face.

"I have my people looking into it. With gate travel outlawed, you understand it takes more than a wish on a star to learn what it is you want to know."

Frustrated, Dan clenched his fists at his sides before forcing himself to relax his hands. Whatever she said, he knew she could open a gate if she truly wanted to. Dragons were creatures of both worlds, and the Cat had some method of communicating to the Otherworld. His mind was too occupied with Abbie's safe return to figure out what game the Cat was playing.

"What do you want in return?"

"Rushing, rushing," she tutted. "So quick to rush into deal making, are we? Very well." The Cat tossed away the file folder, smoothing out her pink pencil skirt as she stood. "You could just give me a blank check, as the humans might say."

She winked at his stony face.

He stared at her impassively. "You know that an open-ended deal isn't an option. You will not trick me."

"That's what they all think," she said, not perturbed in the least at his resistance. "You want me to find your daughter for you—in the Otherworld. If I find your little Abigail, you will take one of my people with you to the Otherworld. I assume you plan on opening a portal to her location." The Cat walked around him, her bare feet silent on the dark hardwood. "Or had you not thought that far ahead, little one?"

He straightened, seeming to grow larger as he took the hand she trailed across his chest and firmly put her aside.

"I am Wodan, Lord of Summer, Leader of the Wild Hunt." He focused on her dragon eyes. *"You will not question my abilities."*

The Cat smiled slowly, her eyes glittering. "Once upon a time you were, but fifteen years of exile do things to a man. Or an elf, whatever you are now. Without access to your magic..." She waved a hand sadly. "No portal. I will not open it for you, as it would break my own deals with the Seasons. If you have no plan to get her back other than to beg a dragon to do it for you, then we have no bargain."

Dan's body flushed with anger at the Cat's flippant words, but he knew she was at least partially right. When the Gates closed, sealing him and his fellows in a world without magic, he had grown soft. But if he had the ability to simply open a portal, he would not be there at all. Only a dragon could draw on their magical abilities in this world...

And so could a changeling.

His mind raced with possibilities. He could force his daughter's doppelganger to open a gate and then—and then he might wander the Otherworld for months trying to find Abbie.

Titania would find him within days.

While he and the rest of the exiled Hunt had made no deals regarding their banishment (and some had even fought to the death to avoid it), their continued stay outside of the Otherworld was the subject of an historic Bargain between the Seasons. Titania would be furious to find him in Summer, and the likelihood of her simply returning him to this world as punishment was extremely slim.

Dan met the Cat's eyes. *She* could find Abbie's location. He could be in and out, and then once back in this world, the Queen could not retaliate.

"I will keep the changeling alive," he said, hating every word he said. "It will open the portal for me and your associate, when you find where my daughter is."

The Cat clapped with delight. "Now *that* is more like it. Very well, Wodan. We have a Bargain." The word weighed upon him heavily as she put out her hand for him to shake.

Wodan took it, and a tingle of deal-magic settled on the pair of them, sealing the accord.

The pediatrician prescribed rest and plenty of liquids for Abbie, as well as a calorie rich meal replacement to get her weight back up. Fiona was torn between relief that the doctor hadn't found anything drastically wrong with her daughter and distress that there was nothing to do but ride out whatever virus she'd picked up.

"I usually feel confident in my ability to diagnose her," she confided to Dan in the kitchen. "Somehow this just ... feels different?"

Fiona ran her fingers through her long hair, twisting it into a messy bun as she looked at the changeling sitting on the couch with her nose in a book. Sammy sat on his cushion in the far corner of the living room, his eyes glued to the girl. When she lifted her head and glanced at him, the little dog leapt to his feet and ran up the stairs.

"She'll be fine," reassured Dan, looking up at the ceiling at the sound of the Jack Russell racing into the master bedroom. "Do you want me to go pick up the Ensure and Pedialyte?"

"If you don't mind? I feel a little run down after running errands with her this morning."

"Not at all," he said. "Go sit with her. Relax." Dan gave her a little push on the rear, and she swatted at his hand as she walked out of the kitchen. He watched as she sat on the couch beside their daughter—no, *not* their daughter. Dan rubbed his forehead, imagining a headache was forming. Abbie snuggled into Fiona's arms as his wife took the book she'd been holding and began to read aloud.

He stared at the ring of keys hanging up by the phone and pulled his driving gloves out of their drawer. Fiona stretched her face up for a kiss as he made his way out, and his lips tingled as he walked out of the house, reluctantly leaving the changeling to feed on his wife.

CHAPTER 9

Into the Steelwood

"ARE WE THERE YET?"

"Not yet."

"But how much longer?"

Abbie swiveled her head to look at the forest surrounding the group. Trees and more trees. It was like wading through an endless sea of branches, and they'd been walking for days. Okay, a day and a half. She was a sturdy girl, but she was by far the shortest person in their group and keeping up with Nadiene's long strides proved difficult.

"A few more days." Nadiene looked at Abbie and paused until she caught up. Foster remained in the rear, looking cautiously around as they took a breather. "Unless you know of some horses we can use."

Abbie shrugged. She slipped her pack off her shoulders and flopped down on the ground next to it.

"Can I eat something?"

Nadiene grimaced above the girl's head, her fists tightening, and Charles stepped smoothly between her and Abbie. He knelt beside her as she struggled to open her bag, offering to help with a smile.

"Perhaps a little jerky? It is a long journey, girl."

"I know," she sighed, accepting the strip of dried meat the thieftaker took from her rations, trying to summon some enthusiasm about it. "And we're closer to the border than we will be to the center of Winter when we cross it. You told me already."

"Any magic we use beyond what hides us from the wolves could make us more visible to others." Charles patted her head, and she took a bite out of the jerky with a bit of a struggle.

"A little break will do us all good," he added, looking meaningfully at Nadiene, who rolled her eyes and turned her back on him to stare into the trees. He turned back to Abbie. "How are you holding up? Feet hurt at all?"

"I'm okay," she shrugged.

Her new boots were actually very comfortable. She'd been a little worried that they wouldn't be, remembering stiff new shoes back home, but they were somehow soft and sturdy at the same time. Charles had experimented by the campfire last night, showing her how she could stuff them with fur to keep her toes warmer once they crossed into Winter. He was also teaching her how to stitch some of the furs together onto her cloak with a big wooden needle and a strand of waxed linen thread. Abbie smiled up at him as she chewed the jerky until Nadiene interrupted.

"We should move on," she said abruptly, reaching past Charles and picking up Abbie's pack.

The big man stood up, concerned.

"What is it?"

"Something is behind us," the wolf replied, her voice hushed. She gave him a warning look, and he pulled Abbie to her feet.

Abbie shouldered her bag once again, and they set off at a faster pace than before. She found herself panting as they dodged between the trees.

"Is it the wolves?" she whispered loudly, and Nadiene shook her head without looking back.

Relieved, Abbie hitched up her pack and concentrated on not tripping over any roots as she hurried after the grown-ups.

Foster studied the trees, analyzing the way the leaves danced in the warm breeze.

"We are upwind."

Abbie felt the tension growing in her little group. Even though she had no idea what might be happening, her own stomach tied up in knots. Nadiene shrugged out of the straps of her pack and handed it to Charles. The big, bearded man slung it over one shoulder, pausing a step so he could walk beside the girl.

"I can smell them," said Nadiene sharply, looking back at Charles while her hands worked on loosening the ties of her leather wrap shirt. "They are making an attempt to be quiet, it seems."

He nodded, looking down at Abbie, who considered reaching for his hand.

"It will happen quickly," he said in a low rumble. "Be brave."

"What will?" she whispered.

They kept a steady pace. Abbie looked over her shoulder at Foster, who appeared to be trying to look everywhere at once.

Nadiene released a strangled sigh, and Abbie's head whipped around just in time to see the dark-skinned woman collapse to the ground. Her hands hit the dirt first, only they were no longer hands. The girl gasped as a great, shaggy brown wolf shook itself free of Nadiene's clothes and loped off through the trees to the left. Charles paused mid-stride only to pick up the discarded garments and stuff them haphazardly into her pack.

"The Steelwood is near," he said, eliciting a soft cry of alarm from Foster. "We will walk toward it—and when I tell you, child," Charles looked down at Abbie, "Run."

"Can't we hide?" she whimpered, the strangeness of the situation hard for her to process.

They continued through a brightly lit summer forest, the trees far enough apart one could see for a good way in either direction. Daisies and other flowers grew in clumps in the underbrush. There was a lot of *stuff* growing between the trees, now that Abbie considered it.

"They would wait us out," said Foster, just loud enough for Abbie to hear him.

"Who?" asked Abbie.

He turned to face her, his eyes wide with fear.

"Goblins," he said.

"There," said Charles, pointing with his chin.

Abbie caught sight of a bush shaking thirty feet or so away from them as they walked forward. Her mind tried to guess what these goblins might look like but came up short.

"The Steelwood is straight ahead," Charles continued softly. "If you continue in this direction. Pick a tree in the distance and run toward it. Once you get to it, pick another in the same direction. Should keep you from getting turned around."

Abbie nodded, her brown eyes wide. Charles kept on at his steady pace, laden with two packs but strolling effortlessly.

"Pick your tree, Abbie. Got it?"

She looked ahead of them, focusing on a tree with slightly darker bark, and nodded.

"Good." His hand dropped to his sword hilt. "Run!"

Abbie darted forward like a frightened rabbit, a cry stuck in her throat. Foster yelled as Charles dumped the packs on the ground, a bronze, leaf-shaped sword in his hand as the under-brush erupted with green bodies. Abbie couldn't look back. She could only run forward as fast as she could, her wild stare fixed on the tree she ran toward.

"Back! Back!" yelled Foster, hands out, a flash of vines growing up and enveloping one of the larger goblins. Green-gray, bulbous-bellied with stick-like arms and lumpy features, the goblins threatened them with wooden spears, sharp teeth, and ragged claws.

Charles swung his sword, neatly cutting the tips off the nearest goblins' crude spears.

"There are quite a lot of goblins," he said. "Unusual!"

"What?" asked Foster, incredulously. The big human seemed almost joyful as he slashed and cut at the smaller, but quite numerous, goblins. The elf tried to focus on his magic, coaxing more cooperation from the forest around him. Plants tangled the feet of more of the creatures, causing them to fall and be trampled by their fellows as Charles and Foster backed up the way Abbie had run.

The goblins had attacked quickly and silently, and the monstrous creatures continued to merely murmur as they swarmed. A ragged shriek from the back of their ranks split the air, and Foster caught sight of a sleek back and tail as a goblin was thrown into the air, bloodied. Charles yelled and attacked into the front of the creatures, his sword spilling brownish blood that smelled like the underside of a troll's foot. Foster snatched up a thick-stemmed daisy, snapping it from the plant with a breathed apology, and aimed it wildly as a goblin leapt at him.

A bright greenish light, magic drawn from the element of Earth, shot forth from the flower, channeled through it as the boy concentrated as much as he could. The energy blast punched the goblin backward in mid-air, and it squealed as it tumbled against a tree trunk.

"That's how we do it!" shouted Charles, but his enthusiasm was hampered by his enemies being so much shorter than he was. He had the advantage, but the goblins kept coming, and it was all he could do to keep the monsters from surrounding them. "Nadi!" he yelled, pointing out a group of the swamp-dwelling creatures that were breaking off and heading after Abbie.

The wolf bounded through the underbrush, tearing through the goblins as if they were paper dolls. Her thick fur offered protection from their scratch and bite, and she was too quick for them to turn around and get their spears in place. She fell upon the splintered group like a vengeful demon, the strength of her jaws snapping bones.

Abbie kept running. She could hear the others fighting behind her as she picked out her second tree on the run, dashing around bushes and jumping oversized mushrooms as she dodged trees and kept running in the same direction. Her lungs burned, and she sucked in great mouthfuls of air, her pack jostling against her back as her legs kept pumping, fear fueling her flight. The noises behind her were like nothing she'd ever heard before, and they filled her with terror for her friends. It was hard to stay on her target as she worried, her mind jumping from one frightening possibility to the next, but she managed somehow.

Charles's shouts grew even quieter as she picked out a third tree. What was the Steelwood, and how would she know when she'd reached it? Was she even still going in the right direction? *Is Foster okay? Did the goblins kill*—She squeezed her eyes shut for a moment, desperate to stop the awful thought before it finished. Abbie slowed to a fast walk, unsure if it was better to keep going or to stay within earshot of her only friends in the Otherworld *who were definitely fine and not dead.*

She'd looked away and was now trying to pick her destination tree out again, but she wasn't sure she'd found it. Abbie gulped, continuing forward. All she saw were trees, now growing thicker and blocking out more of the sun overhead. Fewer plants grew underneath in the shadows, but there were more mushrooms, their bright white caps almost glowing against the mulched earth.

She glimpsed a bright gleam tangled in the roots of a great elm up ahead, silvery in a rogue sunbeam. "The Steelwood?" she wondered aloud. The distance muffled the sounds of the fight, and she almost felt safe as she walked toward the shining thing in the ground, her breath slowly easing.

Something bumped her in the middle of her back, and Abbie gasped, whirling around to face a big, lumpy green goblin as tall as she was. Its yellow eyes narrowed as she put her hands out to ward off another poke with his blunted wooden spear. "You come," it said, chapped lips parting to reveal its brown, stained teeth.

When she hesitated, it jabbed with its spear once more, and she backed up hastily. "Come," the goblin gurgled, but there was nothing inviting or reassuring about it.

"N-no," Abbie stammered, and another goblin popped out from behind a tree and then another. The first—and largest—one snatched at her, and she screamed.

A radiant brown wolf, Nadiene, erupted from the undergrowth, leaping at the goblin, teeth flashing as she snarled and bit. The goblin stumbled backward, bleeding, but another darted forward, knocking the wolf backward with the butt of its spear. Nadiene yelped, scrambling for purchase in the detritus of the forest floor as the goblin spun its spear around and stabbed downward.

"No!" screamed Abbie, thrusting her hands forward in fear and desperation. The goblins didn't even have time to look surprised as a great gust of wind whipped through the trees and blasted them backward. Abbie turned and ran, past the strange, twisted steel figure trapped in the roots of the elm and deeper into the Steelwood.

The undergrowth was nearly nonexistent there; only grass confronted her feet as she ran. She knew the goblins were picking themselves up off the ground and coming after her. She didn't look back. She was too afraid of what she would see if she did.

Abbie darted around a tree, too terrified to be amazed at the suit of armor nestled in its roots. One elm grew around another set of steel armor, holding it nearly upright—almost as if the tree had pulled a knight directly into its trunk. The girl ducked under a gauntleted hand and zig-zagged through the next few trees, desperately looking for a place to hide. She could hear goblins running behind her, communicating to each other in grunts and garbled shouts, and she pounded on a tree trunk with a closed fist. "Open. Open!" There was no response.

She dared a glance over her shoulder to confirm that the goblins were closing in and ran again, deeper into the Steelwood. There was no cover. She knew the goblins were getting closer, and she was getting too tired to keep running. Abbie threw herself on the ground behind a large elm, scrambling into the hollow made by its roots, which was hardly a hiding place at all.

"Hide, hide, hide," she whispered, squeezing her eyes shut.

She was sitting out in the open, her back against a tree trunk. The goblins made their way through the Steelwood; she could hear them muttering back and forth to each other, but they were slow in their progress. Abbie cracked an eye open and found herself staring at the empty eye sockets of a skull. The bones grinned at her from inside a suit of armor tangled in the strong wooden roots of the tree, and she gasped. She dragged her eyes away from the macabre sight just as the first goblin came into view.

It crept through the forest, giving the trees a wide berth. She was sure it looked right at her as it turned its head back and forth, but the air around her shimmered slightly and its bulging, sallow eyes slid away from her as it continued to stalk through the grass.

Another goblin slunk by in the wake of the first; this one was the large fellow who had spoken to her. It bled from a cut on its head, crude spear still in hand but used more like a crutch as it hobbled through the Steelwood. Abbie cringed as a third suddenly appeared, this time on her right and close enough that she could have reached out and touched its filthy foot as it rounded the tree she pressed against. It smelled like rotten meat and moldy bread, and she put her free hand over her nose, trying not to gag.

Why didn't they see her? She stared at her hand. *Did I... use magic?* First the wind, and now she was somehow invisible. The thought thrilled her, but the danger was still so close she couldn't relax. It didn't really matter *how* she was hiding, it only mattered that she *was.*

Can't we hide? she'd asked. *They will wait us out,* Foster had said. But maybe the goblins would just keep pacing forward, searching for her.

"Can smell you," said a goblin, a small one with a great mop of mossy hair falling into its eyes. More goblins filled the Steelwood in front of her, but they were moving slowly and carefully picking their way around the trees. None touched the fallen warriors' armor. Abbie spared a glance to the skeleton at her side and saw that it was clutching a sword that appeared to pierce through the tree's trunk. If she moved quickly enough, she might be able to knock its hands from the weapon and grab it for herself—if it wasn't stuck fast inside the tree. It would be noisy. If it didn't work, she would have given away her hiding spot to the fifteen or so goblins that surrounded her tree.

The creatures were almost silent as they moved, lumpy and gangrenous looking, but they barely stirred the grasses as they began to circle around. "Know you are here," rasped one of them as it looked blindly around for her, walking closer and closer. She tore her eyes away from the goblins, focusing on the sword. One quick grab and pull—like the sword in the stone. The sword in that story, of course, could only be pulled by one person.

But then, I guess I have magic now, right? Abbie waggled her fingers a bit, but nothing seemed any different. A goblin and its flaring nostrils were walking past her only steps away, and she accidentally shifted against the tree. Abbie blanched as the goblin turned its head directly toward her, and she knocked the armored hand off the hilt of the sword with a clatter.

Her fingers hurt as they closed around the metal, but she turned and took the hilt with both hands, yanking with all her might. The sword slid free, the lack of expected resistance sending her onto her back, the weapon tip arcing over her head and lodging in the torso of the goblin. Abbie gaped up at the creature, black blood spurting onto her face as it squealed and gurgled. With a tug, she pulled the sword free and rolled over, the weapon resting in the grass as she pushed herself up onto her hands and knees. The other goblins turned and rushed toward her as she scrambled to her feet, the sword heavy in her hands as she raised its tip to the canopy.

A flash of bright white seared her eyes and she flung an arm up to shield them as something flew toward her and smashed into the next closest goblin, knocking it off its feet. Abbie tossed her head around, gaping wide-eyed as what appeared to be giant icicles peppered the Steelwood. The goblins screeched and ran around in circles; Abbie crouched down as the icy barrage continued.

The ice made an indescribable sound as it arced through the air: a cold, deadly sound, and when it ended, the silence was deafening. Abbie gritted her teeth and peered ahead, brandishing the sword in front of her as she searched for the source of the attack. Perhaps it had saved her, but it could be some other threat, someone else who wanted to take her to the Summer Queen. Or eat her. Or both?

When the figure finally emerged, he was tall and pale, long silvery hair sweeping back from an aristocratic brow, and she backed up against the tree again, the wood firm and reassuring. Abbie held up the sword, trying her best to look fierce even as its weight strained her arms. "Stay back!" she yelled, and the man stopped, standing between two trees twenty feet away. He looked at her intently from head to toe, his hands spread slightly as if to show he held no weapon. His clothes were white leather embroidered with ice blue and pale green thread, and she knew he must be a Winter elf.

"I am at your service." The elf bowed deeply and elegantly, his voice soft and musical. "Gwyn app Nudd. I knew your father."

CHAPTER 10

There's No Place Like Home

WHEN A STRANGER introduces themselves to a child, saying that they know their parents and that it's perfectly fine that they come with them or talk to them or go see their puppy, children are taught to view this with skepticism. Yell, run away, find a safe adult to stay with (preferably your actual parents); do what you need to do, but under no circumstances are you to go with the stranger or believe them. When the child has fallen through a portal to the Otherworld is chased by creatures who wish to turn her over to the elven Queen of Summer, and the stranger is an elf who couldn't *possibly* know her father, such an introduction is terrifying.

Abbie slid around the side of the tree, rough bark catching on her shirt as she backed up farther, the sword she'd pulled from its trunk gripped tightly in her hands.

"You don't know my dad," she said fiercely, the sounds of the retreating goblins growing fainter behind her. Where was Foster? Or Charles? Or Nadiene?

"I wish to speak with you, Abigail." He said the name as if he were tasting it, testing it out for the first time. "It *is* Abigail, is it not?"

She took another step backward, the tree still to her right. "You can't know my dad. Don't lie to me. I'm a kid; I'm not stupid."

"Be careful!"

Abbie took another hurried step back and caught her foot on a root. She sprawled in the roots of the tree, the sword falling beside her as she painfully landed on top of the steel armor. Her skin felt like fire where she touched the metal, and she scrambled to roll off it as fast as she could. Tears sprang to her eyes, blurring her vision, and she reached for the sword even as Gwyn knelt at her side.

Cool hands helped her sit up, but she wrenched herself free from them, dashing the water from her eyes. "Be careful, child. Iron is not kind to us." He looked around and then back to her, focusing. "You are already recovering," he said, wonder in his tone.

Abbie rubbed at the red rash on her hands and arm, feeling a similar patch on her back where her shirt had pulled up and exposed her skin to the armor. "What do you mean, 'iron is not kind to *us*?'"

"It is deadly to the Fae." He studied her face from where he knelt, now out of arm's reach as she scooted backward again, more carefully this time.

"I know that," she said rudely, a half-remembered bedtime story from her father bubbling up in her mind. Abbie stared at the slowly fading allergic reaction on her hands. "But it doesn't kill *me*."

Gwyn scanned the Steelwood. There were no further sounds of goblins, but they could be stealthy when they wanted. "Your father, Wodan, he does not touch iron, does he?"

"That's not his name, and he's allergic, like me." Abbie found the sword hilt with a questing hand and dragged it closer. The elf chuckled but stopped when she glared at him.

"Your skin does not blister and crack because you have a human mother. I assume, at least," he said. "Your father was exiled from here, the Otherworld, many, many years ago. He was a friend," Gwyn added. "The blood of an elven lord runs through you, Abigail, no matter what name he goes by now."

She stared at him without blinking. He was talking nonsense; he *didn't* know what he was talking about, or he was outright lying to her to try to gain her trust. But she *had* just summoned wind to protect herself and somehow hidden in plain sight of a bunch of goblins.

The Winter elf nodded, watching her face as her thoughts ran through her mind. "You can feel what I am saying is true."

"Hey!" A shout echoed from over her shoulder and made Abbie break eye contact with Gwyn as she caught sight of Charles running toward her, eyes blazing over his ginger beard. The Winter elf stood smoothly, standing a safe distance from the girl, his hands spread palm up.

"You have nothing to fear from me," he said, his face as calm as ever, even as the big man galloped up beside Abbie.

Charles reached down and helped her up, a flicker of glee crossing his face as he saw her sword. All business again, he pointed his own bronze weapon at the intruding elf. "Be on your way, and you'll have nothing to fear from me."

Gwyn laughed, then said, "Oh, you *are* serious. Well then." He turned to Abbie. "I only want to help you. It is what your father would want."

"What's he talking about?" asked Charles, glancing down at her.

"He says he knows my dad," she answered in a small voice. "That I'm part elf, too." She tugged on her regular, human ears self-consciously.

Gwyn smiled faintly. "Ah, a half-elf's ears may be pointed," he gestured to his own elegant ears, pulling his silver hair out of the way. "Or not. Sometimes they change as the half-elf grows older. I am telling you the truth, Abigail."

Abbie scowled, dropping her hand to her side. She was only called Abigail when she was in trouble, and she didn't want this guy to say her name anymore. "I don't believe you," she said in a small voice. "I just want to go home."

"How are you even here?" Charles asked the elf. "I am surprised the wolves did not come down on your head the moment you crossed the border."

The Winter elf smirked. "The border is only secure to a point. If *you* attempted to cross, no doubt that would be the case. I have a little more… finesse."

A great brown wolf padded through the forest behind Gwyn, a low and throaty growl causing the elf to turn around. Abbie nearly sighed with relief to see Nadiene appear uninjured.

Charles quirked an eyebrow. "Perhaps you don't have as much finesse as you'd like to think." Abbie looked up fearfully, edging behind the big man, and he looked down reassuringly. The wolf bared her teeth in a snarl, and the Winter elf backed away, his hands slowly raising.

"Hands down," said Charles softly. "She'll bite them off before you can get a spell off." He put his hand out for Abbie's sword. "May I?" He offered his own in exchange, and she gave up her hard-fought prize for the bronze weapon, which would be much easier for her to hold. Charles walked closer to Gwyn, pausing when he was just opposite him to toss a bundle of leather in front of the wolf. She caught it in her great jaws and stalked behind one of the bigger trees. Abbie's eyebrows raised at the strange, fleshy sounds emerging from the tree but the ensuing standoff between Charles and Gwyn quickly distracted her.

The Winter elf bristled. "Carrying *that* is a capital offense, boy."

"What?" said Charles, innocently. "This?" He hefted the steel sword, giving it a bit of a spin in his hand. Abbie didn't know much about swords, but it was long and shiny and the bearded man held it as if he knew what he was doing. "There's no one here but us. Who would question an elf killed by steel in the Steelwood?"

Gwyn flinched, his cheeks gaining a bit of pink as Charles spun the sword around again. "I mean the girl no harm. I came specifically to find her and offer her my protection."

"She doesn't need your protection." Charles narrowed his eyes and gave the sword one more bounce before leveling it at the elf.

"Don't!" Abbie ran and put herself between the two adults. Once she had their attention, she faltered. "He kept the goblins from getting me," she said uncertainly. "You can't kill him 'cause he helped me. And… he said something about my dad."

Charles looked down regretfully at the sword and lowered it slowly. The Winter elf relaxed, but only a bit. "Girl, the elves say many things, but they are always lies." His eyes hardened as he looked at Gwyn over the top of her head. "Trust me on that."

"He knows my name," Abbie countered.

"He knows your name? *I* know your name—that doesn't mean I know your father."

She grimaced. "But… he still helped me."

Charles looked over his shoulder. "Foster! Hurry up!"

Abbie looked, too, surprised that she hadn't been worried at the boy's absence until now. She caught sight of Foster picking his way very slowly through the Steelwood toward them. His sun-browned face was pale, but he lifted an arm in acknowledgment of Charles's shout.

"He will be here soon enough," said Nadiene, emerging from behind Gwyn, no longer in her wolf form.

The Winter elf turned smoothly to face her, but just enough so he could keep Charles and the steel sword in his line of sight.

"You must be mad to be here," said Nadiene.

"In the Steelwood?" Gwyn asked, his mouth twisted in amusement.

"In Summer," she said calmly.

"Wait!" interrupted Abbie. "What's my dad's name?"

"Wodan," said the elf. "I said as much already, child."

She sagged a little. "That isn't right."

"See?" said Charles, lifting the sword once more. "A liar."

Nadiene gave the Winter elf a sharp look.

"Wodan can't be the girl's father." She frowned, but Abbie could tell that something had changed. "What is your name, elf?"

"Gwyn app Nudd."

He made to bow but stopped short as Charles lazily shifted the sword. The elf stood stiffly, no trace of his sardonic smile. Nadiene sucked in her breath at his name, and her bearded companion looked at her.

"What is it?"

"Do you not know who this is?" she asked urgently.

Abbie said hesitantly, "I did magic, so maybe he is right."

Charles didn't seem to hear her.

"Besides an arrogant, sanctimonious arse? I mean—that's all elves though. No offense," he said over his shoulder to Foster, who'd just arrived.

"None taken," Foster said faintly. His blond curls stuck damply to his sweaty forehead as he took in the scene. "What is going on?"

"I was invisible," Abbie said, wondering if she was somehow invisible again as everyone continued to ignore her.

"This Winter elf claims to have saved Abbie from the goblins. What's more ridiculous is his claim that he knows Abbie's father," said Charles.

"He says he is Gwyn app Nudd, and that the girl's father is Wodan," said Nadiene.

"What?" shouted Foster. He abruptly sat down and put his head in his hands.

Gwyn caught Abbie's eye and winked. She scowled at him.

"Who is Gwyn app Nudd?" Charles asked, impatience rising in his tone.

"You have heard of the Wild Hunt?" Nadiene asked.

"Yeah, but that was disbanded years and years ago." The big man looked from the wolf to the elf then back again. "Wasn't it?"

"Of course it was," she said. "And the Hunters were banished from Faerie, lest they grew restless and tainted the peace between the Seasons."

"Is that what the story is?" interjected Gwyn, drawing a frown from Nadiene. He held up his hands in mock surrender.

"I still don't get it—oh. Oh...!" Charles's face sputtered through a variety of expressions like rifling through pages in a flip-book. "Gwyn and Wodan are the names of the Hunt's leaders from Winter and Summer. So what you're saying is… what are you saying?"

"They were banished," said Foster, back on his feet again with a little more color in his cheeks. "He is lying. He cannot be who he says he is."

"My dad's name is Dan," said Abbie. "And I did do magic."

Once more, they talked over her. "We were not *all* banished. The Queen of Air and Darkness protected me. My role was more... complicated than a mere Hunter."

Nadiene snorted. "You are saying the Horned One was sent away, and you were kept back?"

"There is nothing worse than Summer's sudden storms," Gwyn said cryptically. "With Winter you know what you are in for. All this is ancient history, of course. *Why* things are the way they are is less important than *what* they are. I am *here*; Wodan is *there*. And I will see his daughter safely back to him."

"Who is his daughter?" asked Foster, still trying to catch up on the conversation he had missed due to his slow and paranoid walk through the steel-infested forest. "Wait, what?"

Everyone started talking at once until Abbie stamped her foot.

"I DID MAGIC!" she hollered. The sudden silence was deafening, and she put her fists on her hips. "I blew away a bunch of the goblins before I ran into the Steelwood. Nadiene saw."

"And she pulled off an impressive glamour spell as well, especially for a beginner," said Gwyn. "Hid herself completely from sight."

Foster's mouth fell open, and he sat down again, his leafen clothes changing color slightly to match the browns and greens of the ground.

Now that she had everyone's full attention, Abbie took advantage of it.

"Can humans do magic here?"

"No." Nadiene slowly shook her head, her face unreadable.

"And elves can't do magic in my world?"

"Nope," said Charles, regarding her thoughtfully.

Abbie fingered the rounded tips of her ears again.

"My father's name is Dan. That's like Wo-dan." She looked at one of her hands, as if it were about to sparkle with visible pixie dust. "So could it be true? I'm... part elf?"

"This might be a troubling realization," said Gwyn smoothly, still wary of the steel sword Charles carried. "But yes, you have both the blood of a human and the blood of an elven lord running through your veins."

"*Coooool.*" Abbie turned her hands over again, examining them. They looked the same as always. "That's awesome." She caught Nadiene's eye and hesitated. "It's awesome, right?"

The dark-skinned woman finally nodded.

"A half-elf is rare, and you will have many abilities in this world that you cannot touch in your world. Reacting with awe is... appropriate, I suppose." She shot the Winter elf a look across her hawkish nose that Abbie couldn't quite parse.

Charles faltered with the sword, unsure whether he should put it down or not. Gwyn took a step back and to the side, sidling out of his immediate reach.

"The Queen doesn't know. Our Queen," Charles added as the Winter elf raised a perfectly shaped silvery-white eyebrow. "Or your Queen...?"

"The Queens are unaware. Grandmother Winter can scarcely sense her own borders this time of year, and the Lady of Summer likely thinks Abbie is just another Lost Child."

Gwyn eyed Charles meaningfully. Abbie caught the glances as they shot over her head, back and forth between the adults, but it was hard to keep up with what they were *saying*, let alone what they might mean between the lines.

"Do not worry," said Foster from the ground. "Rather than simply enslave you for life, now you will be put to death."

"What? They'll kill me because I'm here?" Abbie looked around, and Nadiene nodded solemnly. She focused on Foster then pounced on him, grabbing him by the front of his shirt. "This is all *your fault!*"

Foster weakly fended off Abbie's attacks until she dug her knuckles into his ribs, then he shoved her off him. Angry tears welled up in her eyes, and she dashed them away, pushing herself to her feet.

After a moment, she put her hand out to Foster. The Guardian-in-training sighed and took her hand, accepting the help up off the ground.

"Are you still going to help me?" she asked him.

"Of course I am," he bristled. "I told you I would."

Foster smoothed out the front of his shirt, still unnerved by where they were standing.

"And are *you* guys still going to help me?" Abbie asked, a little less fiercely as she looked up at Charles and Nadiene.

"My resolve is unchanged," said Charles without hesitation, planting the tip of the sword into the dirt and lightly leaning on the hilt. "I will see you to Winter's Gate."

Nadiene regarded her bearded companion, but she nodded as well.

"I, too, will assist you, Abigail," pronounced Gwyn, unperturbed as everyone stared at him. He smiled faintly, adding, "If you will allow me to, of course."

She studied him, her brown eyes scrutinizing his light blue ones. The silence stretched for half a minute until she spoke.

"Okay," she said.

Amused, Gwyn repeated, "Okay?"

Nadiene scowled but said, "We should keep moving. The goblins may return, and in greater numbers."

Charles nodded. "The Steelwood will slow them down, but if they get the idea to surround it, we will be trapped." He paused a moment before gesturing grandly. "After you, Gwyn app Nudd."

If he knew that he was being asked to go first just so everyone could keep their eyes on him, the elf did not show it.

"Gladly," Gwyn said as he set off through the wood, picking a path that gave the armor-infested trees the widest berth. Charles discarded the borrowed sword at the foot of an elm with great hesitation but kept his hand on the hilt of his own sword as he followed behind the Winter elf. Abbie and Foster stepped quickly behind the taller adults while Nadiene brought up the rear.

Abbie reached out and took Foster's hand, almost reflexively. The touch reassured her. When he looked at her in surprise, she said, "I'm glad you're okay."

The elf boy hesitated, then squeezed her hand gently.

"I am glad you are okay as well."

"I am fine, too. Thank you for inquiring," Charles boomed, looking over his shoulder with a wink.

Abbie giggled. There was no further talk until the group had cleared the Steelwood and its graveyard of armor-encrusted skeletons.

CHAPTER 11

Into Winter

THE DYNAMIC AROUND the campfire changed with the inclusion of Gwyn. He sat slightly apart from the others, not nearly as close to the small fire. The group had enjoyed a nightly routine, but Abbie sensed an awkward shift after the aristocratic Winter elf had joined them. Damp from a scrubbing in a nearby stream, Abbie munched on a handful of berries and stared at him from across the flames.

Gwyn caught Abbie's gaze and stared back without blinking. She glanced away sheepishly to find Nadiene's eyes on her as well, so she returned her attention to the fruit in her hand. Foster sat down near her. Abbie looked sideways at the elf boy, and she scooted closer to whisper, "Do they really... *kill*... people like me?"

Foster hesitated, then shrugged.

"There have been no half-elves for at least a hundred years. Several hundred, perhaps. I am new, comparatively, born just twelve Summers ago. If the wolves caught you and brought you to the Queen, I could not say what she would do." He failed miserably in his attempt to be reassuring.

Abbie set her jaw firmly and turned her gaze to the small fire, watching the flames flicker and jump.

It isn't my fault, she thought. *I didn't do anything—and now there are people who want to kill me?*

Abbie had vague notions about death, having gone through a period of existential dread when she was six after understanding the concept of people she loved becoming dead, but the thought of being *killed* was different. Would it hurt a lot?

"Try not to think about it," said Foster, and she looked up. "Anyhow, Charles has sworn to keep you safe."

Abbie could feel the corners of her lips turning down as an image of the boisterous thieftaker set upon by enormous wolves took root in her mind. Abbie gave her head a little shake and took a deep breath to chase away the wretched thought. Refocusing, she realized that she could be scared, or she could keep working forward to her goal. She felt a stab of loneliness and pride as she thought of her mother. Her mother never gave up at her job. No matter how difficult the birth, she would figure out a way to fix the problem. Abbie could almost hear her mother assuring her. *It doesn't matter if it's hard; it matters that you keep trying*, she would say.

Allergic to iron or not, Abbie closed her eyes, found a bit of emotional steel inside herself, and gripped it tightly.

"How about a story?"

Abbie opened her eyes, surprised to hear Gwyn's voice. He was still watching her from across the fire, but his face had softened, and his smile seemed kinder. He glanced toward Nadiene for approval, and the wolf shrugged.

"What kind of story?" Charles asked, looking more interested than anyone else at the camp. He adjusted the plump birds he'd hunted for dinner over the flickering fire.

"The story of the Steelwood." Gwyn's eyes met Abbie's as Charles shrugged. "She has not heard it."

Abbie thought for a moment. "Is it a true story?"

"As true as we can know," the Winter elf said. "It was many, many years ago, centuries of seasons, and the story has probably grown in the telling." He raised his eyebrows and winked. "Or perhaps it has shrunk."

Nadiene snorted her disinterest, but Abbie leaned forward expectantly. Satisfied he had an audience, Gwyn settled in.

"Many years ago, the Steelwood was just another patch of Summer forest. The dryads would cavort there on clear evenings, dancing with elf and faun alike, while the Wee Folk perched in the branches. Unbeknownst to them, in the human world, there was a great amount of unrest. The Wild Hunt regularly trampled through their carefully laid out kingdoms, stirring up wars in their wake as they chased the Boar.

"A German king was heartbroken when his oldest son was swept away in the Hunt. His son was caught up into the Hunt with the Horned One and the Harbinger as they ushered in the change of Seasons. It was known that humans could be cursed to become part of the Hunt as it passed, and it was unfortunate that the prince was taken so. The king grew old waiting for his son's return, and as he assumed his son had been killed, he plotted an attack on the Otherworld as revenge. He sent his strongest knights to kill a dragon for its blood, giving the prize to a witch so she could draw up a portal to the Otherworld just outside his castle walls. He assembled his armies, gave his younger son his blessing and command, and sent his soldiers and their steel armor into the land of the Fae.

"Only one returned through the portal, hours later, his eyes wild. The men had all been killed, including the king's younger son. The old King, with a heavy heart, ordered the witch to close the portal, lest any more Fae creatures find their way through. He died as it closed, his heart broken from the loss of his sons.

"The very next day, the older prince returned, having not aged since the day of his disappearance. He took up the rule of the kingdom in his father's stead. This is the story they tell in your world."

Abbie cocked her head to the side. "I've never heard it before."

"It is the story they *would* tell in your world, then," adjusted Gwyn smoothly. "What the old King never knew were the details of the battle on *this* side of his witch's portal. As the armored knights and foot soldiers entered the Otherworld, it was like poison seeping into a paper cut. Their iron made them almost untouchable, but the Queen of Summer knew she must sacrifice her subjects to stop the invasion. She dispatched a Guardian to the part of the forest where the knights poured in through the gate, and he woke the trees—not to dance but to battle. The great elms of the wood screamed as they attacked, dying even as they killed. Dryads are not naturally aggressive, but the Guardian pushed them into a frenzy. The trees enveloped the humans, pulling them to pieces, strangling them—"

Gwyn halted his story when Nadiene threw a stone at his arm, and he took in the sight of Abbie's and Foster's eyes, both as large as saucers. He grinned.

The wolf frowned. "They defeated the invasion. We all have seen the aftermath; there is no need to supply gory details."

"A Guardian would never do that," said Foster. "We are the defenders of the forest." He shuddered.

"And what better defense than to keep such a terrible invasion from happening?" Gwyn shrugged. "You saw the Steelwood for yourself. A graveyard for human and dryad alike."

Abbie latched on to one of the other details of the story.

"The old king opened a portal with dragon's blood. Is that part real?"

"Yes," said Gwyn. "That is true. Dragons are very powerful creatures from the Otherworld." He frowned lightly. "Of course, it is *all* true—"

"So if I kill a dragon—" said Abbie.

"Hold on," interrupted Nadiene. "First, we are not killing a dragon. Second, even if we could find a dragon, there's no way to get them to do what you want. It would have to *want* to help you."

"But the old king in the story…" Abbie raised her eyebrows and looked pointedly at Gwyn.

The Winter elf was nodding along but started when Nadiene fixed her gaze on him. They shared a look Abbie missed, before he blurted, "Of course, in the *story*, but he had a witch, and there are no witches here."

"Oh." She paused, disappointed, until another thought occurred to her. "But you all perform magic all the time!" She jabbed a finger toward Foster, who recoiled from the suddenness of it. "That's how *he* brought me here!"

Charles cleared his throat.

"Abbie, you know we can't dial up a gate to send you home. Ever heard of Rip Van Winkle? No? Well, he messed around with unblessed gates, and when he *did* get home, it was one hundred years after he'd left. Everyone he knew was dead. Better to stay in the Otherworld than to do something like that."

Abbie's face fell, and she tucked her knees under her chin, wrapping her arms around her legs. Were her parents even looking for her? Foster said they wouldn't be, that they would be fooled by a changeling. But she was sure they'd know it wasn't her. Wouldn't they?

Sleep that night was scarce, and Abbie at last fell into a restless dream. She was in a room, or perhaps a house, the walls covered with funhouse mirrors that stretched and squashed her reflection as she turned this way and that. The more she looked for a way out, the longer the hallways stretched in front of her, twisting and turning until she was hopelessly lost in a labyrinth. Something was following her. It looked like her own reflection appearing and then disappearing beside her in the creepy mirrors. But the footsteps… they followed her everywhere she ran.

She woke up sweaty, her heartbeat slowing as she took in her surroundings and left the dream behind. Her companions stirred as the sun rose, and Abbie tried to put thoughts of the mirror maze and the stalking creature out of her mind. Still, she found herself looking over her shoulder more than once as they broke camp.

Gwyn offered to lead the way to Winter's border, but Nadiene staunchly refused, so the two spent much of the journey side-eyeing each other. Flat forest transitioned into rolling hills, but they stuck close to the trees and far from any established paths. Sometimes at night or in the early morning, Abbie would wake up to the sound of wolves howling in the distance. One night, she caught Nadiene sitting up, listening in the light of the moon. The wolf turned her head toward the girl, and Abbie closed her eyes quickly. Walking all day was exhausting and, despite her efforts, pretending to be asleep meant she was soon actually asleep again.

Foster tried to show her how he laid the notification and protection wards around the camp, but apparently the element she was gifted in was not compatible with his. Earth and Air were opposites. If she concentrated, she imagined that she could see *something* as he moved his hands.

"The symbols we use for the wards are from the old elven language," Foster explained, his fingers drawing a series of loops. "It is just to focus the mind, however. The elemental powers do not know English or Elvish... or rather, they know all languages. Are you listening, Abbie?"

Abbie guiltily looked away from Charles roasting dinner and nodded.

"Yeah. Kinda."

She pinched her eyebrows together in concentration as the soon-to-be Guardian continued.

"So, Earth magic encompasses Ground and Forest. My specialty is Forest: the green, living aspect of Earth magic." Foster brushed his hands down the front of his shirt, all made of soft leaves that never wilted. "I made my clothes as part of my initiation into the Guardians."

"What are you going to do about your offering for the Queen?"

Abbie hadn't forgotten that he'd been trying to complete an entirely different quest while helping her get home.

The older boy's shoulders slumped, and he dismissed the magics he'd been drawing up with a wave of his hand.

"I do not know yet. I... will know it when I see it."

He stared at her for a long moment, and then he looked away, the tips of his ears turning pink.

Abbie impulsively squeezed his hand.

"It'll be great. I just know it. Maybe in Winter you can find something awesome. I bet none of those other Guardians have ever been there."

She was right, Foster knew. No Guardian had ever crossed the border—or if they had, they had enough sense to keep it to themselves. Traveling into Winter was not breaking the truce *technically*, and if their team disturbed nothing and avoided all Winter elves, so much the better. Foster found Gwyn in his eyeline and blinked. Avoided *any other* Winter elves, he amended in his mind.

Their journey that day took them to the Border. Abbie felt a mixture of excitement and dread in the pit of her stomach as the surrounding woods took on their autumn colors: a band of the riotous oranges, reds, and yellows. The group trudged through the fall tones a few hours longer as they approached Winter.

They paused among a stand of birch trees for Nadiene to scout up ahead. She smiled at Abbie as she left, her scar pulling at her face in a way that was no longer frightening but familiar. As the wolf disappeared past the papery trunks, Abbie looked up into the golden yellow leaves overhead, the trees sighing in the cool breeze.

"It is not necessary." Gwyn shrugged as Charles frowned. "I told her the path was clear. I have at least a *little* skill in hiding my tracks. I am a Hunter, after all."

"Was," grunted Charles. "You *were* a Hunter."

Gwyn's eyes cooled, the icy blue frosting over.

"Of course. Yet, your Summer Queen has not set her dogs on me, nor has the Guard arrived at our location. You can trust me." He looked at Abbie, who watched the exchange. "I have her best interests at heart."

"We'll see," rumbled the big thieftaker.

Charles did not go so far as to give voice to his concerns that there could be an ambush waiting for them—on either side of the border, for that matter. Nadiene would sniff out any threat, quite literally.

"You have your warm clothes ready?" Charles asked Abbie.

Abbie nodded, opening the top of her pack to show him where she'd folded the wool cloak. She had carefully stitched the warm rabbit fur Foster had brought from Berryhaven into a lining, and they had winterized their boots with more fur.

Gwyn sniffed with disdain at their preparations for the cold conditions. "I can help with that," he'd said a few times over the last couple of days. "But only once we are in Winter. I cannot throw magic around on this side. More than I have already, of course." He had winked at Abbie, leaving her feeling uncomfortable.

"Good," said Charles, his voice bringing the girl back to the present. "Just a bit longer."

Charles turned his head in the direction Nadiene had gone and scratched his beard thoughtfully.

Foster turned in place, looking back the way they'd come. His home, and his former purpose, seemed very far away.

"Foster, your clothes!"

Abbie pointed at the elf's leafen shirt, amazed that it was changing color to match the surrounding foliage.

Foster looked down at himself blankly.

"Oh. Right. It's a spell used by the Guardians." He fingered the bottom of his shirt, brushing his thumb over the orange leaves. "For camouflage," Foster explained absently, before he returned to staring off in the direction Nadiene had left. The closer they got to Winter, the more the Summer elf seemed to retreat into himself.

Abbie sighed. Everyone was preoccupied with the border crossing, but she tried not to think too much about it.

A movement caught her eye, and she froze. A slight figure passed between the tree trunks in the distance, giving Abbie an impression of light brown skin and golden, leafed hair. The woman wore a white papery dress, and she paused a moment to stare back at the girl before walking behind another birch tree and disappearing. Abbie's mouth fell open and she caught Foster's eye.

"Um, dryads are nice, right?"

"They are nice, and not nice, just like everyone else," said Charles. He looked around them at the trees. "They tend to stay to themselves. The larger the group passing by, the more likely they are to remain sleeping."

"So they're sleeping?" She followed Charles's gaze up toward the trees. "Not... spying?"

"The trees hold no particular loyalty to either season," said Gwyn, even though no one had asked him. "They may tell of our passage if someone comes along, but they are just as likely not to. I would not worry about it. There is nothing we can do, either way."

"We are moving every day," added Charles. "If anyone is even on our trail they will be far behind, thanks to Foster's woodskill."

Abbie reached out a hand and reverently touched the trunk of the nearest birch, her fingertips lightly brushing the smooth, white bark.

"Trees belong to themselves," she said.

Foster met her eyes, a grin spreading across his face. Abbie grinned back.

Nadiene rejoined them.

"The way ahead is clear. It is a good place to cross—as good as any, anyway," she added, before Gwyn could say anything smug about his advice.

"Good enough for me," said Charles, pushing up to his feet.

Abbie walked in the middle of the group, her pack on her shoulders as she tried to see around Charles's burly body. Twisting her head around, she noticed Foster lagging behind. She motioned for him to catch up, and he quickened his pace until he walked alongside her. *He is afraid of leaving Summer behind*, she realized.

"It will be okay," she whispered.

"I know," he said, but it didn't sound like he believed himself.

Abbie nearly walked into Charles's back. He had stopped suddenly, and when she peered around him it became clear why.

They had arrived at the border.

The trees were splendid in their fall colors, an explosion of foliage worthy of any painting, and they continued beyond the seasonal border. Pines and firs mingled with the maples and oaks, the forest thinning until only the evergreens remained. Snow coated the ground a few yards ahead, piled against the trees in drifts, and Abbie imagined she could feel the cold emanating from it. On this side, however, the clover was green and lush. Birds sang in the distance, and she could still hear crickets chirping.

"Cloaks on," reminded Nadiene, and Abbie put her pack down to prepare properly for Winter.

Once they'd all dressed in their extra clothes (except for Gwyn, who watched them with amusement), the wolf tugged at Foster's arm, pulling him to the edge of Summer.

"Take a look… please," she said. He cast a glance over his shoulder to Abbie and then stared into Winter. The breeze stirred up the loose powder, but the snow never blew into Summer, pressing against the border like the inside of a snow globe. "We want to sneak past the wards without taking them down or setting them off."

"Right." The young elf closed his eyes for a moment, running one hand through his curly, blond hair. After a moment he opened them again. "*He* got through," he said, gesturing toward Gwyn. "Maybe we should—"

"*He* was one elf, alone. We are a larger group. Concentrate."

Foster sighed, drawing on Earth to feel out the wards. Nadiene raised her head, nostrils flaring as she scented the air for danger. In bipedal form, her senses were not as sharp, but they were still superior to that of either an elf or human.

Abbie stood near Gwyn, who observed the wolf and boy with interest. He looked down and caught her staring, but she didn't glance away.

"Watch this," he said, walking up to the border a few paces from Nadiene and Foster.

Charles shifted his stance as the Winter elf clapped his hands twice and blew across the border as if he were blowing out a candle.

The air rippled, and Abbie gasped as symbols glimmered in front of Gwyn and spread out like a glowing spider web. Beyond them, through the snow-covered trees, something huge started to move.

CHAPTER 12

Cat's Cradle

THE CLOCK TICKED slowly to the next minute, and Dan forced himself not to look at it. *Abbie is still missing. That thing is not Abbie.* It was a mantra he repeated to himself, over and over again.

The changeling looked at him with her wide, innocent eyes as it lay in bed, curled up and sweaty. It grew sicker with every day that passed. Dan was having trouble keeping Fiona away from it and justifying to his wife his own distance from his supposed daughter.

"I just don't understand what's wrong with her," said Fiona quietly in the kitchen over their morning coffee. She scrubbed a hand over her face, her fingers lingering on her temples. "At first I thought it was the flu, but the test was negative. Whatever it *is*, we haven't caught it."

"We've been careful to minimize contact," he pointed out, and her mouth twisted up a bit.

"That sounds so clinical," she said. "But yes, we've been careful. And she isn't getting any better." Her lips tightened into a line, the way they did when she was holding back tears.

"Hey, hey, it'll be okay." Dan put his hand over hers, and she took in a deep, shuddering breath, turning her face away. "She's going to be okay," he repeated. *Because I will find her.*

Fiona just nodded, and Dan leaned in close, brushing her hair out of her face and kissing her forehead. He gathered up their empty cups and took them to the sink. It was getting harder and harder to keep his intelligent wife from rushing their "daughter" back to the doctor—his Fae abilities were severely stunted in this world, but he worked with what he had.

"I'm not going to the clinic today," Fiona said. "Well, I am, but just for one appointment—high-risk mama I need to see myself. Dr. Lieber is going to cover the rest of my patients." She looked at her watch, dabbing at her eyes with the cuff of her other sleeve. "Can you get Abbie her breakfast?"

"Of course." Dan watched his wife pull herself together. "Are you taking some vacation time?"

"No—yes. I *should* be," she said, the guilt she carried suddenly a ragged edge he could almost see. "It's just the day for now. The Ensure I bought should help her put on weight." She looked into the distance, her eyes losing focus as she formed her own mantra to hold on to. "She'll be okay."

"I truly believe it," he murmured, breaking the moment by opening the fridge, the condiment bottles rattling as the door swung open.

Fiona blinked, looked at her watch again, and grabbed her purse.

"I'll see you in a little bit," she said, and then she was gone.

Dan looked at the little white bottle in his hand and took it upstairs. He had to keep the thing alive so it could open a portal, but meal replacements weren't going to do it. Keeping it away from other children was the most important thing for now, but that was easy enough to do when it was so sickly.

Outside her room he braced himself, then quietly opened the door and stepped inside.

"Good morning," he said, and "Abbie" moaned in that way she would when she didn't feel good and didn't want to wake up. "Got your breakfast."

He helped her sit up, brushing her long brown hair out of her face from where it had escaped her braid. The changeling dutifully sipped at the Ensure through a straw, making the same nose wrinkle Abbie always did when she was tasting something she didn't really like. It broke his heart to see.

She was noticeably thinner than she had been, and for a child with no extra weight to begin with, it was a startling change. She caught him looking at her and stopped drinking.

"Am I going to be okay, Daddy?" she asked, and Dan blinked.

Abbie is still missing. That thing is not Abbie.

"You're going to be fine," he said, gently putting the straw back into its mouth. "Drink up. This will help you get stronger."

The little girl focused on the meal replacement, drinking with extra seriousness. In the old days, when the conflict between the Seasons was at its height, changelings were more commonly found. If a baby fell ill suddenly, failing to thrive, the parents suspected their own, healthy child had been stolen by the Fae and replaced with the sickly changeling. Dan had heard of entire villages laid waste by a changeling's magical powers if it was nurtured and brought to full health. Thus, the mythos of the changelings grew, and people found harsh ways of dealing with them. Abandoning the child in the woods was a frequent solution—the changeling child would die, though the parents' real child would never be returned. Sadly, they sometimes punished innocent human children as well, unsure what to believe. *Was it the exposure to the elements that killed the changeling, or simply being alone?* Dan wondered.

He had never seen one up close before, but it was hard to think rationally about the one in front of him. At times, he wanted to throw the creature out the window, but guilt would follow on the heels of such thoughts. Whatever it was, it was a child. Or rather, it *appeared* to be a child.

Abbie is still missing. That thing is not Abbie.

From time to time, he felt a surge of Fire magic when he touched it. Other than a tingle, it didn't seem to affect him. Dan tried to think with cold logic, but it lead him to a choice he didn't want to make. Changelings were magical creatures created by the elves. He was an elf. It could not sustain itself with his essence.

Distracted by his thoughts, he was caught off guard when the changeling snuggled against him. Reflexively, his arms wrapped around her, muscle memory from years comforting his beloved child, and for a moment he held the girl close, breathing in the scent of her clean hair.

Abbie is still missing.

He pushed her away as gently as he could.

"You need to rest. Just sleep for a while, okay?" Dan checked the bottle of Ensure, smiling encouragingly when he saw it was empty. "Do you want a banana or something else to eat?"

"No, thank you, Daddy," she said.

Her face was drawn and pale, with just two spots of color in her cheeks. He leaned her back gently into the bed, her bones easily felt through her shrinking muscles. Something would have to change, or there would be no changeling left to open a portal for him... and the Cat's associate.

He was waiting at the front of the house when Fiona came home, folding her into his arms in an encouraging embrace.

"She's sleeping, but she ate."

"Sleeping again?" Fiona looked up at the ceiling where Abbie's bedroom was while Dan kissed her forehead. "I'm so worried…"

It was a startling admission from Fiona. Dan tightened his arms around her.

"It'll be okay. I promise." He pushed what magic he could muster into his words, willing it to be enough.

"You can't promise things like that," she murmured into his shoulder, but she relaxed a little before wiggling out of his hug. "Right," she said, pulling a mother's strength onto herself like armor. "It's your turn to get out of the house. You've barely left since she got sick."

"Bu—"

"No buts, really. I took time off so I can be here, and you need time off, too." Fiona stretched up and kissed his cheek. "Call a friend. Get a drink."

He looked at the clock. "It's not even eleven o'clock."

"Okay, maybe not a drink," Fiona smiled. "Go on now. I've got this."

Dan ended up in an old diner, walls covered with faded photographs, just before lunch time, waiting on a friend to arrive. There weren't many he'd held on to over the years—it had been a decade at least since he'd contacted anyone from his old life. Harold, or Harry as he was known now, was someone he knew he could always call on, mainly because the man owed him.

"Dan, is it?"

He looked up and grinned at the speaker.

"Harry." Dan got up, shaking the man's hand. "And your hound, I see."

The dog at Harry's side looked up, unimpressed at the reunion.

"Never go anywhere without him," Harry said, clapping Dan on the shoulder and sliding into the booth. The dog laid down on his feet with a sigh. "I was surprised to hear from you. Been a while."

"I wish it was under better circumstances."

"Problems in paradise?" Harry motioned the waitress over and ordered a coffee. She eyed the hound, but it was wearing an in-service vest, so she said nothing.

"Changeling," Dan said.

His old friend's eyebrows raised. Dan quickly ran through what had happened.

"That *is* a problem," said Harry, shaking his head as he took in the story. "Going to the Cat is a desperate move, and she knows it."

"Well, I am desperate," he said.

"And her associate—any idea who that might be?"

"No. At this point, I don't think it matters. Whoever it is, I'll hold up my end of the deal, as I have sworn."

"Of course you will," agreed Harry. "Isn't much fun being saddled with a magical creature now, is it?"

Dan's eyes tracked down to where the hound appeared to be sleeping. "Well…"

"Oh, do not make that face," laughed his companion. "We have buried the hatchet, as they say. Sure, I was upset after the first few days, especially when it turned out to be a couple hundred years…"

"It was not me," said Dan, not for the first time.

"I know it wasn't. The point is, I know what it is like to have a family—and to lose it." He sipped his coffee. "Ancient history."

"I never appreciated how much that… what it feels like." Dan glared into his own drink. "Being here… it has made me appreciate your kind much more than I thought I could."

"She's a half-elf," Harry said, matter-of-factly. "You know what that means, over *there*."

"I do."

Harry made a non-committal noise through his nose and drank some more coffee, obviously refraining from continuing the thought to its logical conclusion. Dan bristled.

"She's a smart girl."

"She's eight," his companion replied mildly.

"She's either fine or she isn't," snapped Dan. "Until I know which it is, there is no use dwelling on a bad outcome."

Harry shrugged. "You are right, of course."

Dan shook his head. "I'm deluding myself." He rubbed a hand over his face. "Look, get what you want for lunch. I'll see you around."

He dropped a couple twenties on the table and scooted out of the booth, Harry and his hound watching him go.

Wodan walked for an hour, aimless, just trying to clear his head. Dwelling on what he *couldn't* do was driving him mad. He flexed his fists, digging his short fingernails into the meat of his palms. He would tear apart heaven and earth to find Abbie, but here, *here*, in this place, he was practically powerless. If the changeling hadn't shown up, perhaps he would never have known what had happened to her.

The impotence of his exile stung deeply, cutting him to his quick. Perhaps this, finally, was the Queen's judgment on him. A removal of the last bit of himself, of what made him who he had been. He felt useless in his inability to hunt down and find something that meant more to him than the Great Boar ever did.

"You're a hard man to find."

Dan looked up from his memories, one hand still clenched into a fist. One of Cat's men stood near him, but not so close as to be threatening.

"Not really," he said.

"Yeah, not really," smirked the man. "She's got news for you. Wanted to tell you in person."

"News?" Dan looked up sharply. "Is my daughter alive?"

The man shrugged, then his outline wavered, and he disappeared. Dan cursed, checking his watch. He had enough time to get to Cat's downtown office. Fiona had given him the whole afternoon... What was he concerned about? Had he been so neutered by life with humans that he was worried she might be upset he was gone too long? Him, the great Hunter, the ancient Horned One?

Dan picked his cell out of his pocket and gave Fiona a call, letting her know he might be a little late.

Driving to the building was exasperating. Every stoplight took too long to change, and every car was drove too slowly. The building loomed ahead, and he parked on the street, carefully pocketing his keys. Humans littered their entire world with steel and iron—probably a subconscious way of protecting themselves from the Otherworld. Thankfully, the rise of plastics had made the world an easier place for an elf to negotiate, his keys a prime example of a metal object mostly covered with a layer of plastic.

Dan was tempted to take the stairs just so he could run, but after getting past the building doorman, the elevator opened, and a calico cat padded out of it. The cat yawned, stretched, and then walked back into the elevator as Dan made his way toward it.

Looking inside, he found the Cat leaning against the railing, her purple hair draped around her shoulders.

"Come, come, child of the forest." She beckoned him into the elevator with her, and he cautiously entered. They were alone.

She pressed the button for the top floor, leaning back languidly against the side of the elevator as the mechanics sprang to life. A shiny acrylic covered the entire interior of the elevator and the inner rail was faux wood, rather than the ubiquitous stainless steel found in abundance in most modern business offices.

"I'm glad you came as quickly as you did, Wodan."

"You have news?" He didn't feel like wasting time with pleasantries and was glad she didn't either.

"Yes… yes. Such news I have!"

The Cat spoke in a purr, her hand near her throat, and he was suddenly uncomfortably aware of how close she was to him in the confines of the box whisking them upward. Her scent was musky and wild, closer to that of an animal than the woman she appeared to be.

He blinked, forcibly looking away from her and pushing away thoughts of how well her dark purple business suit fit.

"My daughter?" he asked.

"Yes. News of her."

The Cat edged closer to him, her vertically slit pupils boring into his until she was almost touching him.

Wodan put a hand on her arm, gently, and then more forcibly, keeping her at bay with a little effort.

"Tell me!" he growled. She shivered, a smile of delight broadening her face.

"All in due time," she said, trailing a finger up his other arm.

"Tell me now," Wodan gritted out, his hand tightening on her wrist. "I have waited long enough! No more games!"

He pressed her against the side of the elevator, and she laughed as the doors opened behind him. He glared down at her, tempted to keep her pinned until she told him what he wanted to know. A more rational part of his brain reminded him that this was a creature who held a *lot* more power in this world than he did. With reluctance, he released the Cat's arm, stepping back and away from her.

"Well, you don't disappoint," she said, brushing off her suit jacket and pushing past him into her large penthouse office. "Come on. Follow, follow."

Wodan clenched his teeth and then exited the elevator behind her, easily keeping pace behind. She led him back to the pseudo-throne room where she had held court with him the other day, ignoring the large chair on the dais in favor of a set of padded couches in the corner. He sat on the edge of one while she relaxed into the other. After a moment of silence, he leaned forward, his glare set to remind the Cat of his need for answers.

"Ah, yes. Little Abbie," said the Cat, as if she had never stopped talking.

She ignored the thundercloud over Wodan and snapped her fingers. A tall woman appeared from around a corner, bearing a tray carrying two glasses of iced water. When he ignored the offered glass, she set it on the low table in front of him while his host sipped her own. He used the time to study the Cat's assistant. She was built like a tank, tall and muscular, her strength barely hidden in the human clothes she wore.

"She is alive," the Cat finally offered.

His eyes locked on to hers, and a silver thread of tension that had been holding him upright snapped, causing him to sag with relief.

"You're certain?"

The Cat drew up a little, her eyes narrowing. "I will pretend you didn't say that."

"Of course, my apologies." Of course she was positive. It was the terms of the Bargain. Wodan's heart surged and sank all at once. His Abbie was still alive. *She is alive.* A frown flickered over his face. "But where is she?"

"Not captive in either Season, at least not in the traditional sense. Titania does not have her, though it seems She put up quite a search for an intruder in Her realm. There is no word at all from Winter's court either way, and that tells me the sleeping Season cares not at all about her intrusion."

"Her intrusion?"

"Yes, Abbie is in Winter." The Cat sipped her water, the ice tinkling in the glass.

"In… Winter? But why? On her own?" Wodan frowned deeper.

"Oh no, no, she isn't alone. It seems she's gathered a little ragtag group of friends around her. It's quite adorable in its own way. A young Summer elf and a pair of scoundrels. And an old friend of yours."

"A… *friend* of mine?" Wodan was still trying to process how Abbie had gotten a Summer elf to follow her into Winter, though he had an idea of *why* they were doing it. "And what kind of scoundrels?"

The Cat paused again, delighting in drawing out the reveal.

"A pair of thieftakers from Summer. I do not think they see any reward in causing her death, so she is likely safe with them."

"Cold comfort," he replied dryly. "What friend of mine are you talking about?"

"Gwyn app Nudd."

Wodan surged off the couch. "WHAT?"

The Cat watched him, no change in her body language as he loomed over her, clenching and relaxing his fists. As he turned on his heel and stalked a few paces away, she mewled, "Is something the matter?"

"Gwyn is dead. Or... I do not know, but..." He turned to face her again. "He has been in the Otherworld all this time?"

She blinked, her vertical pupils large in the lower light of her office as a slow smile spread across her face.

"I thought you knew. *Fascinating.*"

Wodan found his way back to his seat and forced himself into it.

"Knew that he was not in exile with the rest of us? No. No, this I did not know." He met her gaze. "Why is he there and not here?"

The Cat shrugged.

"Not part of my current investigation. We could strike another Bargain? No? Well then. I think we are done here. Your daughter is alive! Be happy!" Her pleasant expression hardened as she added, "Is your changeling ready to open a Gate?"

My changeling can barely hold its head up, he thought but didn't say. Wodan reined in his frustration and shock at the news of Gwyn, concentrating instead on Abbie. She was in Winter with dubious allies.

"It will be ready. But I have to strengthen it first."

"Life force in, life force out," said the Cat, cryptically. She rolled her eyes when his expression remained blank. "You'll have to feed someone's energy to it. It's been a century since they were in wide use, but surely you haven't forgotten how they work."

Wodan ignored her insult, eager to end their partnership.

"Thank you for the information. I will let you know when I am ready to open the gate."

"Tick tock," she said.

He was keenly aware of the passing time as he made his way out of the building and back onto the downtown streets. He knew that time in the Otherworld could move at a different pace from how humans experienced it. Abbie had been missing for a little less than a week in human time but could have been there for multiple weeks—even months. There was not a moment to waste, and yet he still felt reluctant to do what needed to be done.

When he arrived back home it was dinnertime, and the house was dark and quiet.

"Fiona?" Wodan took the stairs two at a time. "Fiona!"

The door to Abbie's room was ajar, and he pushed it open cautiously. His wife lay in bed with what she thought was her daughter, their cheeks side by side as she slept with her arms around the changeling. For a moment, he considered pulling her away from the creature, but the Cat was right. He walked closer, leaning down to kiss Fiona's forehead and feeling a strange tingle on his lips.

His wife looked pale, and the changeling seemed to be healthier. He brushed her hair out of her face with his fingertips, and then walked quietly out, leaving the changeling to do its work.

CHAPTER 13

Lost Boys

"HEY!" BARKED NADIENE, closing in on Gwyn with a bound, Foster jogging behind her. "What are you doing?"

"Showing the way," he said mildly, unperturbed at her barely restrained anger.

Before them, in Winter, something like a great mound of snow rose from the ground as Charles strode forward. After a moment, Abbie followed him until they were all gathered together, right on the edge of Summer.

"That's an ice troll," said Charles mildly, as snow fell off the creature, revealing its milky white shape. "In case you were wondering."

He looked down at Abbie with a reassuring wink, and she took a step behind him. Nadiene continued to harangue Gwyn.

"You wanted us to come here to this spot, then you wake up the border patrol with your fumbling about! Stop trying to get us killed!"

"I saved young Abbie's life," he said again, calmly, his fingers still twitching in rhythm until she slapped his hands down.

A frown creased his perfect skin, and he looked into the wolf's eyes. "Be careful who you pick a fight with, little one." He seemed to grow taller, paler, and more beautiful as she snarled at him, and then Foster interrupted.

"The, uh, wards are down."

He looked up at Gwyn and Nadiene and pushed his way between them, startling them out of their row. He stood with his toes nearly touching the snow, and then hesitantly, he stepped over.

"If we can go through, that *thing* can do it as well," said Charles with a bit of excitement.

He put his hand on the hilt of his bronze sword. It had been with some reluctance that he had left the good steel one behind, but being caught out in the Otherworld carrying steel was a death sentence.

Gwyn forgot Nadiene for the moment and put his hand on Charles's over the sword hilt.

"Do not draw your sword against him." He strode over the border, his white clothes that had made him stand out in Summer now blending in against the snow. "This is my companion. I left him behind so I could travel without being detected. He guarded this spot against others, on my orders."

For a moment, the rest of them stood frozen on the border. Foster was particularly reluctant to go any farther. But when Abbie ran across, the others followed without further hesitation.

"I can't quite believe we're doing this," murmured Charles to Nadiene as he stepped into the snow for the first time.

"We have a plan, and we are sticking to it," she said. "Forget about him."

Despite her words, she gave the back of Gwyn's head one more glare that might have melted ice.

Foster caught up with Abbie, his breath fogging the air. It was such a strange thing to experience that he exhaled forcefully on purpose to watch his breath rise before him. Abbie giggled.

"Dragon's breath," she said, huffing out a few clouds of her own.

Foster stared with wonder. Whatever he'd been about to say to her flittered away from his mind. The giant ice troll was soon right in front of them as Gwyn app Nudd reached where the creature stood. The troll had not advanced on them, nor had it set off any detectable alarms. Still, it was a powerful Winter being, standing head and shoulders above Gwyn and Charles, as well as impressively wider.

"This is Bryn Bach," said Gwyn, turning to face the others, his back to the huge troll. "He is my *gwas*, my servant, and will not harm you."

Abbie gasped as the ice troll lifted a huge four-fingered hand and rested it gently on Gwyn's head.

Bryn Bach spoke with a voice like ice cracking on a lake, the words unfamiliar except for one: "…friends."

"Yes, yes, friends." Gwyn ducked out from under the hand. "Come on now, you all stick out like spring flowers."

Abbie glanced up at the sky through evergreen branches. The sun was in the same place as before, and as she looked back, she could see the Summer forest as it was: bright and vibrant with colors, insects buzzing about and birds singing. In contrast, the world around her was quiet and still, the snow carpeting the ground in a blanket of white. As she watched, she could see the border wards shimmering back into place and then disappearing.

"Let's go," said Foster, as the Winter elf and ice troll moved farther back through the trees, the troll walking with a grace belied by his size.

Nadiene stalked through the snow with stiff legs and hunched shoulders, visibly uncomfortable, while Charles followed along behind with a smile. Abbie could see what Gwyn meant by sticking out—their dark leathers contrasted with the snow while he had already nearly disappeared. She hugged her fur-lined cloak closer as she walked through the snow.

The snow was only a few inches deep, and Abbie didn't have much trouble following in Charles's footsteps. Foster lagged, surveying everything with a mixture of wonder and suspicion. The cold brought a flush to his cheeks and seeped into his arms and legs despite the warm clothing.

A ball of snow hit Foster in the middle of his chest, and he gasped, trying to prepare a defensive bit of Earth with iced fingers. Then he heard Abbie laughing. She had another snowball in her hand and a mischievous glint in her eyes. Foster stopped walking, and he took a moment to stare incredulously before stooping to make a ball of his own.

"Children!" hissed Gwyn, looking back. Then he sighed while making a knocking motion with one fist. The tree nearest them shuddered and snow fell from its branches, dumping on top of Foster and narrowly missing Abbie. The young elf emerged spluttering, shaking thick snow from his golden curls.

"We don't have time to play," said Charles, taking a few steps back to help Foster shake the snow out of his cloak.

He looked at Abbie as he said it, and she shrank back, ashamed.

"Sorry," she said, looking at her reddened hands. She tucked them up under her armpits.

"Never mind about that," Charles said, pointing with his chin to where the ice troll was disappearing into the trees. "We need to keep up."

"How do we know where we're going?" Abbie asked quietly, hurrying along behind Charles.

"For now, we're following Gwyn." Charles answered. "But if we keep heading toward the center of Winter, we will be fine. Easy enough to find where we're headed. Getting farther from the border before anyone realizes it's been crossed is the main priority."

"Okay," said Abbie.

Abbie looked over her shoulder and saw that the path they were breaking through the snow was slowly erasing, leaving a pristine surface behind them.

"Ice magic," said Foster, walking beside her. "It is a Winter subset of the Water element. Gwyn's doing."

"What is the Winter version of Air?" Abbie huffed out another foggy breath and made Foster smile.

"The Air element for Summer elves—like you, is about lifting, wind, and illusion or persuasion work. Not every Air elf will be able to do the same things with the same element, so there are a few groups, or subsets, of each. You managed to blow some goblins away, and then made yourself invisible, so the things you can do will likely be just in wind and illusion.

"The Winter interpretation of Air is heaviness, fog, and stagnation. Of course," he amended, "I only know about this from what I have been told. Gwyn is the first Winter elf I have ever met... and I expected to meet none, except perhaps at Court. There are emissaries from each Season at the Courts. Ambassadors, if you will. They remain cloistered and do not really go outside. I imagine they are miserable, dealing with the weather."

Foster hugged himself to emphasize his point, his teeth beginning to chatter.

"It isn't that bad," encouraged Abbie, but the cold was biting, making her miss her winter hat, coat, mittens, and scarf. She wanted her mittens in particular—her fingers were reddening from the cold, and she wondered how long it would take for frostbite to set in, causing her fingers to fall off. *Isn't that what happens when you get too cold? Bits start to freeze solid and break off?* She tried to keep her sleeves pulled down over her exposed hands.

The party trudged on in silence for a while. Charles fell back to bring up the rear, while Nadiene remained closest to Gwyn and his ice troll companion. Abbie couldn't quite believe how quietly the gigantic creature moved through the forest, slipping between the large evergreens without so much as disturbing a branch.

Abbie leaned closer to Foster. "Are there dryads in these trees, too? Like in Summer?"

Foster looked up, his eyes focusing on the trees.

"A dryad is not really *in* a tree so much as they *are* the tree, but yes. Summer and Winter have many of the same kinds of what those in your world would call mythical creatures. Like the unicorns I was trying to show you the first day you were here."

Abbie abruptly stopped walking.

"Unicorns?" she squeaked.

"Shhh!" Gwyn looked over his shoulder. "We are almost there."

"Almost *where*?" asked Nadiene, her golden eyes narrowing and nostrils flaring. "I smell… *humans?* A great pack of them."

Charles looked around them curiously, as their little group bunched up on the path.

"I've told you a hundred times, you don't call it a 'pack' of humans. A squall, maybe." He winked at Abbie, who didn't know if he was telling a joke or not. "I see a sign in the trees."

"Sign of what?" asked Abbie, peering up.

"Lost boys."

Gwyn whistled loudly. Bryn crouched down beside him, appearing to be a mound of icy snow, and the Winter forest swallowed the sound. When Gwyn repeated the whistle twenty seconds later, white figures moved into view between the trees.

Abbie couldn't help but feel scared as the beings came closer. Charles had his hand on his sword, but his body remained relaxed.

"Easy," Charles said, sparing a glance for the girl.

Abbie nodded seriously, turning her dark eyes back to the approaching people. They were short and wrapped in white furs, the tallest one walking straight for Gwyn.

"The deal you struck with us is still in effect," the creature said, pushing its hood back. Abbie blinked as she realized it was a human boy.

"Of course it is, and I am bringing part of my Bargain." He gestured to the others, but when no one stepped forward, he turned and fixed Abbie with a look. "Come up, child. You too," he added, as Charles put his hand on the girl's shoulder to stop her from walking. "A human child in need of shelter. Which you are bound to assist, per our agreement."

Charles walked up, a head taller than the teenager speaking to the Winter elf, with Abbie trailing behind him. Foster tried to look in all directions at once and noticed that Nadiene had disappeared.

"This one is no child," said the dark-haired boy, staring sternly at Charles, whose smile split his beard in two.

"Of course he is not, but *she* is," said Gwyn impatiently. "They need proper clothing. *All* of them."

The teen sighed. "That will be for Pan to decide. Very well. But only the humans may follow. The others stay with you."

"Good," said Gwyn. "Great." He looked at Charles and Abbie. "They will provide for you or the Bargain struck will be broken. Do not take too long."

"Very well," said Charles, taking Abbie's frigid hand in his.

They followed the boy through the woods. Abbie was glad that she didn't have to go alone, and that the big thieftaker was coming with her. She had begun to think of Charles as a protective older brother.

The older boy led them onward, winding through the wintery forest, a route that thoroughly messed with Abbie's sense of direction. Charles kept his head up, looking around, and when she copied him she caught sight of a dark shape moving between the trees in the distance.

Charles squeezed her shoulder. "Nadiene," he murmured. "Keeping an eye on us."

Abbie nodded, and from then on she kept looking to see if she could catch another glimpse of the wolf in the snow. She wasn't successful but was distracted from their walk and so, when the boy leading them suddenly stopped, she was caught by surprise.

A tremendous wall of jagged grey stone rose out of the snow in front of them, somehow hidden behind the trees until the last moment.

"This way," said their guide, slipping inside the cliff.

Abbie clutched at Charles's hand, but he led her forward, revealing a wide cleft in the rock, half-hidden behind an outcrop of rock. From most angles, the cliff appeared to have no flaws. The red-bearded thieftaker let his hand linger on the lip of the crack before they followed the boy inside.

"Woah," Abbie said, looking around with wide eyes. The path led them into a small cave with a flaming torch fixed to the wall. The fire flickered and cast their shadows on the walls, the curved entrance to the cave blocking out much of the cool winter sun. The teenager pushed back his hood, his dark eyes glittering in the firelight as he smiled for the first time.

"Welcome to the Cave," he said, stepping backward into the stone wall.

Charles jumped forward as the boy disappeared, and much to his surprise, his hand went through the rock.

"Strange," Charles said, and then he grinned, pulling his hand back out. "Illusion work. I wonder what elf set this up for them?"

Abbie peered at the interior of the cave, unable to see the difference between what was there and what was not. Just as she thought she could see the edges of the fake wall, a hand burst forth, crooking fingers toward them to beckon them through the façade.

"Come on!"

It was the voice of their guide, and Abbie moved forward. She hesitated at the last second, then closed her eyes and stepped through.

Immediately the air was warmer, and light and noise assailed her senses. People chattered with one another—a hub-bub of noise that reminded her of eating at a busy restaurant, sending a pang of nostalgia through her little body. Blinking at her brighter surroundings, Abbie looked over her shoulder and saw Charles on the other side of the illusory wall. From this side, it was merely a shimmering curtain of air, and it was funny to see how he flinched as he came through.

Past the false wall, the space was cavernous, filled with rope ladders and bridges, some with colorful bits of fabric tied on like flags. Children and older teens thronged the Cave, some shimmying up ropes, others dropping baskets of food down from rooms cut into the rock. A large globe at the apex illumi-nated the Cave. Smaller orbs spun slowly around it like moons, drawing her eyes toward a wooden platform built high up in the cave above everything else.

The more she looked, the more she saw. After a few moments, Abbie realized her mouth was hanging open. She closed it with a snap and took a half step closer to Charles, who looked around with a similar reaction. He pointed at the orbs.

"Those are fairy lights."

A crew of kids swarmed around them, all either Abbie's age or younger. She was assaulted by a barrage of questions.

"What's your name?"

"Where'd you get your clothes?"

"Where'd you come from?

The teenage boy who'd led them into the Cave shooed away the other children.

"Leave them alone. Go on now, get!"

The kids scattered, some jumping over a game of marbles played a scant distance away. The boy shrugged at Charles, who still wore a bemused expression. Abbie realized he was the oldest person she could see, and it appeared that fact was not lost on him.

"Where are the adults?" Charles asked.

"No grown-ups," said the teen. "Part of the bargain struck with Pan. Grown-ups don't like games."

It all sounded very familiar to Abbie. Her eyes widened as she took in the Cave.

"...*Peter* Pan?"

"That name sounds familiar," said Charles. "Why do I know that name?"

"Come on," said the teen, leading them through a maze of stacked baskets until they reached another room carved into the cave. "Stay here until I come back. We don't get a lot of visitors."

"What's your name?" asked Abbie suddenly. "I'm Abbie, and this is Charles."

The teen blinked.

"Guy's the name." He pronounced it *ghee*. "Stay here, please. If you need anything, Sarah will get it for you."

A smudge-faced girl a bit older than Abbie stepped out from behind Guy as he turned to go. "Hello," she said shyly. "Are you hungry? Thirsty?"

"What do you do for food?" asked Charles, genuinely curious. "Winter seems a desolate place."

"There is food if you know where to look," said Sarah cautiously. "And Pan provides for us."

"I'm thirsty," said Abbie, and Sarah stepped out for a moment before returning with a wooden cup holding ice-cold water.

Abbie smiled at her as she sipped but then glimpsed Charles who studied the Cave, a serious expression holding his face. When he caught her gaze, he raised his eyebrows and looked out intentionally, then back again. She followed his gaze the second time and saw Guy across the Cave, climbing a rope ladder to a platform about twenty feet up. He walked across it, caught another rope, and climbed that too, reaching higher and higher. Abbie realized he was making his way to the platform just under the ceiling. Was that where Pan was?

Minutes stretched into an hour, and the curious children had scattered, either to play or do chores. Sarah wove a basket nearby, and Charles looked like he was taking a nap, leaning up against the wall with his arms folded and his eyes closed.

Abbie was alone with her thoughts. *How is Foster doing, out there in the snow?* It was so warm and bright in the cave that it was easy to forget the winter landscape outside. Abbie had taken off her cloak and folded it haphazardly into a makeshift cushion she could sit on. Her eyes kept tracking up to the high platform. It was dripping with colorful streamers. In fact, there were bright colors everywhere; the walls were even painted in places with summery pictures: flowers, vines, and bees.

The children all wore white, though it was rare to see someone completely clean. Abbie noticed how they could pull up the cowl necks of their thick shirts over their nose and mouth and put their hooded cloaks on to blend in against the snow outside. In fact, she knew they could disappear, as she'd seen some of them seemingly come out of nowhere when Gwyn had whistled for them.

Sarah brought warm stew with winter carrots and potatoes and a flat hunk of bread that was slightly bitter. "Acorn bread," she said, watching Abbie's expression. "It takes some time to get used to it."

Charles was already sopping up the remains of his stew with the bread, having come back to full alertness when the smell of food reached his nose.

"How much longer are we going to be here?" asked Abbie.

Sarah looked confused. "You aren't staying?" Her eyes flicked uncertainly toward Charles and back again.

"We are just here for better clothes. For us... and for our friends outside."

The older girl quickly put it together. "They aren't human." Her eyes ticked up toward the ceiling almost involuntarily.

Abbie thought to herself, *I guess neither am I, even though I still* feel *human. I guess. Right?* She shrugged instead.

"They're our friends."

"Guy is talking to Pan. I'm sure he will be back soon to let you know what is decided."

Sarah stood up, collected their empty bowls, and slipped away.

With a full belly and in the warmth of the Cave, Abbie found it hard to keep her eyes open. She scooted over to sit beside Charles, copying his position leaning against the wall. It wasn't nearly as comfortable as he made it look, and she was soon leaning against his side, her eyelids drooping.

Voices woke her up before she realized she'd been asleep.

"The clothing is spelled," Guy said. "It will keep you warm and dry." He hesitated before adding, "We do not have anything big enough for you, Charles. This cloak should serve you well, however."

Abbie sat up, rubbing her eyes, and the boys quieted for a moment.

"I thank you," said the thieftaker, "and your protector. This is quite generous."

"It is what we Bargained with the son of Nudd." Guy shrugged, crouching down and handing Abbie a pile of clothes. "Pants, shirt, and cloak. It will only grow colder and colder as you near the center of Winter."

"Thank you," she said. "And there are clothes for Foster too, right?" Abbie yawned, slow to cover her mouth. *How long had they been in the cave?* She wondered. *Was Foster okay, out there in the snow?*

"There are," he nodded. "Your Summer elf friend will not die from the cold."

Guy's tone seemed to suggest that there were a hundred other things that could kill Foster instead. Abbie frowned, and Charles laughed, which only deepened her frown.

"Come now. We must bring these to the others. Get changed, Abbie," he said, pointing to a curtain hung across a section of the cave.

Abbie scampered over. There were three small beds made up on the ground behind the fabric drape, and Abbie tried not to step on any of the blankets as she hopped around to get into her new pants.

The white clothes were a little dingy, but they smelled clean, and Abbie already felt warmer. She twisted her hair as if she were going to tie it into a ponytail, stuffed it into the back of her shirt, and pulled the cloak on over top. Her bow tying was a little messy, but she confidently secured the cloak with a double knot before rejoining Charles. He wore a similar cloak, stitched together out of arctic furs with the whitened leather on the outside. It didn't completely cover his brown summer clothes, but it would have to do.

"Come," said Guy. "We will see you back to your friends."

Abbie craned her neck as she followed the teen, trying to take in and remember everything about the Cave before they left. One of the fairy lights near the ceiling moved out of its orbit, and she watched it float down a few levels before stopping on the edge of a walkway. She blinked, and the light dimmed and resolved into a petite male figure. She almost blurted "Tink!" but held her tongue at the last minute.

This *wasn't* like the stories, and she'd met fairies, the Wee Folk, already in the Otherworld. He seemed somber, and perhaps a little larger compared to the others she had met.

Pan watched them until they passed through the illusory wall that marked his territory and into the outer cave entrance.

CHAPTER 14

Prince of Summer

"I HAD THE strangest dream." Fiona yawned as she poured coffee into a mug, and Sammy pressed up against her leg in the kitchen. "Abbie was outside, and a tornado was coming. The twister was bearing down on her and I couldn't run out and grab her. I was just standing inside, watching it happen through a window." She shuddered, her slim fingers wrapping around her steaming mug. "Awful feeling. I've had a pit in my stomach ever since I woke up."

"Sounds terrible," Dan agreed, looking at her carefully. "Are you okay?"

"Yeah, I'm okay. Just a dream, right?" She sipped her coffee. "I took today off as well. I think Abbie looks better this morning. Do you think so?"

"What? Oh. Yes, she had a little more color in her cheeks," he agreed. *And you have less.* "You should sit with her on the couch," Dan added. "I'll take Sammy for a walk, and you... just relax with her. She needs her mother."

"Okay," Fiona said mildly, squeaking in surprise when he pulled her into his arms as she walked past him. "My coffee!"

He deftly plucked the mug from her hand and set it on the counter, pulling her closer. She playfully struggled for a moment, and then wrapped her arms around him as he breathed in the scent of her hair.

"I love you," he said.

"I know." Fiona kissed him, surprised at the sudden burst of passion as he held her even tighter. "I love you, too."

After a few moments, he released her, planting one last kiss on her lips. "Enjoy your day of cartoons and cuddling."

She laughed ruefully. "Oh, I will. Been looking forward to this."

Dan watched her retrieve her coffee and settle into the living room with Abbie. Fiona pulled a fluffy blanket around them both and tucked the girl under her arm.

He called the terrier over and clipped the leash to his collar. "Come on, Sammy. Let's go for a walk."

The dog wagged his tail happily, as eager as Dan to get out of the house.

It had been a while since Dan had walked in the woods. Usually he was with Abbie, showing her what plants could be eaten and which ones to avoid. She'd become a passable tracker already, and one day she had trailed a raccoon by its tracks in the wet dirt back to its den. She knew most of the birds in the area by sight and song and could start a fire without a match.

She is alive. Dan smiled, but it faded as he remembered *where* she was. If she were in Summer, then her skills could help her.

In Winter, she was vulnerable.

But why is she in Winter? Dan ducked under a branch, his feet on the narrow trail that led into the forest from his back gate. Abbie had come from this trail—rather, the changeling had—so he followed it deeper through the trees, Sammy trotting along beside him. He tried not to think about Fiona cuddling up to the creature on the couch. The early summer forest was cool and damp, and the sky was clear. Wodan looked back over his shoulder, his house out of sight as the trail curved away from him.

A fallen log looked like an inviting place to sit, and he saw paw prints in the dirt nearby. The ground had been soft mud at one point, and Sammy must have walked through it. A child's footprints mingled with the canine ones, toes clearly defined in most of them. He smiled wryly. She was always taking her shoes off, despite Fiona's wishes.

There was a small hollow under the log, where it looked as if something had been pulled out and through the pine needles and leaves. Wodan peered into it, finding a couple of dog biscuits hidden under some decaying leaves. Sammy immediately shoved his nose into the leaves and started in on the treats, his stubby tail wagging happily.

Wodan let the dog sniff around the log and pushed up to his feet, following Abbie's trail. She had shoved through the brush in another direction than she usually went. Had she been following something? There was no sign of other footprints. As he went, he checked the firs for any unusual clefts or deep holes in their roots. Nothing.

A stand of tall foxgloves blocked the way, but he parted them and pushed through, emerging in a clearing with Sammy at his heels. A pond lay in front of him, the sun reflecting on its still waters, a large willow tree overlooking it. Dead wildflowers, now browning in the sun, surrounded the pond.

Wodan crouched down, lifting one of the wilted flowers with a finger before plucking it and giving it a sniff. The plants had most likely begun dying about a week ago. He discarded the flower and stepped through the browned vegetation to the edge of the pond. Some ferns along the edge were still green, but most were on their way out.

Sammy sat down at the edge of the clearing and whined, refusing to walk through the dead plants, or to come any closer to the pond. Wodan dipped his hand into the cool water, frowning.

 He was sure this was where Abbie had encountered a gate. The magic used from the other side would have powered the portal, but the creation of the changeling had sapped the life force from the clearing.

He was still at a loss as to how, or even *why,* a gate had been created. Gates were explicitly against the law of the Fae, as far as he knew. Of course, his information was outdated by decades. Still, it wasn't likely that the Queens, Titania and Mab, had changed their minds about portals into or out of their realms. To maintain the truce between the seasons, the large seasonal Gates were each opened just once a year on the Solstices to release the Great Boar and maintain the balance.

For the first few years of his exile, Wodan had still tried to hunt the Boar, but in this world, the Boar appeared in a different place every time. Without elemental magic, it was impossible to keep up.

Now, stripped of nearly all his magic, Wodan dipped his fingers in the water again. He could still sense the residual effects of the Fae gate, but the pond seemed normal enough, if a little stagnant. The odor of death seemed to linger about the place.

There were no dead fish floating in the water, though whatever *had* been there had no doubt died when the changeling appeared. The vegetation had been killed off to give it life, and whatever had been in the pond had similarly been sacrificed.

Sammy whined and then barked, edging into the clearing.

Lips pressed into a grim line, Wodan peered up at the willow tree. It alone seemed untouched by the death that had come to the clearing. He walked around the pond in an ever-expanding spiral until he found what he was looking for: a small circle of white-capped toadstools, large enough for someone to sit cross-legged within.

He paused and marked the location in his mind. A Faerie circle would come in handy in the next few days.

Wodan whistled for Sammy and the dog joyfully joined him, eager to leave the area.

Hold on, Abbie. Daddy's coming.

The next morning, Fiona wasn't next to him in bed when he woke up. Dan sleepily patted the spot she usually slept in, and then sat up, blinking the sleep from his eyes. A quick sweep of the house revealed her in Abbie's bed, with the little girl tucked up under her chin. His first impulse was to snatch the child out of the bed like a hot coal, but he stopped himself, turned around, and went downstairs to start the coffee.

A few minutes after the coffee started percolating, his wife padded downstairs, led by her nose into the kitchen. He poured her a cup, and she leaned against the counter, inhaling the steam coming off the mug with her eyes closed. When she opened them, Dan was surprised at how bright and blue her eyes looked. After a moment, he realized that it was because her face was drawn and pale. The skin under her eyes had thinned, revealing more of the purplish color of the blood vessels underneath.

"Good morning," he said, pouring himself a cup of coffee, partly to give himself time to come to terms with the shocking change in Fiona's face. He sipped it and burned his tongue, grimacing as he turned to face her again.

"Blow on it first," she chided him gently, and he smiled in reply. "I couldn't sleep," she continued, setting her mug aside. "I just… felt like Abbie *needed* me. So I slept with her." Fiona rubbed her eyes a little, and then pushed her hair out of her face. "It's breaking my heart how sick she is."

Her voice trailed off as she stared at the back of her hand. Dan focused on it as well, noting a tremor, and how visible the veins were. He stepped closer, taking her hand and kissing it, as if that were why she'd been holding it out.

"I am sure she will get better soon."

Fiona sighed, leaning into him and resting her head on his shoulder as he wrapped his arms around her.

"I pray you're right."

"Of course I'm right. She's been—staring at us in the doorway," he finished, turning their bodies slightly so Abbie appeared in Fiona's line of sight. The girl looked brighter and stronger, and she watched them with fascination.

Fiona stood up straight, a smile on her face.

"Oh, good morning, sunshine!" She turned to set down her coffee and crouched down near Abbie. "How are you feeling?"

"Hungry," said the girl, leaning in close and rubbing the tip of her nose against Fiona's just like Abbie would have. They both laughed.

Abbie is still missing. That thing is not Abbie. "Cereal?" asked Dan, already reaching for a bowl.

"Yes, please." Abbie clutched at Fiona's hand, drawing her over to the table to sit with her.

Dan's wife gave him a helpless look, then winked and kissed the top of the girl's head, pulling her chair close and snuggling her while Dan poured Cheerios and milk.

"Your breakfast, m'lady," he intoned, presenting the bowl and cup.

He brought over Fiona's coffee with another flourish, and they both giggled at his antics. Though he felt like he were dying inside.

A little while later, Fiona met him upstairs, a fresh cup of coffee in her hands.

"She's still eating—her second bowl! I told her to take it easy, but apparently she has her appetite back."

His wife looked pleased, but it was hard for him not to notice the pallor of her skin and how the little crow's-feet in the corners of her eyes had lengthened. *Life force in, life force out.* He thought about the glade in the forest, full of dead and dying plants.

Fiona went back downstairs to check on Abbie, and he went through the motions of stripping the beds and gathering the laundry. His days had become full of mundane chores as he transitioned from construction work to house husband after Abbie's birth, but he hadn't minded. Now, for the first time, it grated on his nerves.

Am I becoming soft? Am I lacking the hard edges I spent centuries honing while leading the Hunt? He stared down blankly at the sheets in his hands, methodically bunching them up and shoving them into the washing machine. He'd made changes in order to survive in this human world, and he had never lost himself until Abbie. She had changed him.

For the better.

He didn't start the washing machine. Instead, he walked through the house until he found Fiona and the changeling cuddled up on the couch. The little girl pressed her forehead against his wife's, staring into her eyes with her little hands on Fiona's cheeks.

"Hey!" he said, alarmed at the vacant expression in Fiona's eyes, pulling the changeling off her. "Not so fast!"

Abbie fell into the cushions on the other end of the couch, eyes flashing a bright green as her little face twisted in anger. Fiona blinked and looked up at Dan, startled.

"What the heck, Dan?"

The changeling's eyes flickered between the two parents, and then she screwed up her face and began to cry.

"She's... still sick," he said lamely. "I just don't want you catching what she has."

"She's on the mend," retorted his wife, scooping up Abbie into an embrace and smoothing her hair as the girl sobbed and clung to her. "If we were going to catch something from her, we would have already."

"I didn't mean to—I'm sorry. I just..." He let his words trail off, unsure how to mend things with his wife without tipping his hand to the creature in her arms. "I haven't been sleeping well," he said truthfully, scrubbing his hand through his hair and then over his face.

"Maybe you should go rest," Fiona said, not unkindly, as Abbie quieted down in her arms.

"Maybe I should," Dan said, loath to leave her alone with the changeling. He sat down next to them, the little girl looking at him from where she was nestled against Fiona's body. "Come here, Abbie. Daddy's sorry. You're okay, right?"

She nodded hesitantly, peeling herself away from his wife and letting him hug her. He again felt the tingle of a failed magical connection as he pressed his lips to her forehead, and the girl quickly struggled out of his arms and back into Fiona's.

Wodan got up and left the room.

I am a prince of Summer, he thought. *I am the Horned One, the Leader of the Hunt. And I am undone by a woman and a child.*

CHAPTER 15

Broken Path

"TRY AGAIN. YOU have almost got it."

Foster looked as encouraging as he could while covered nearly head to toe in warm clothes with only his eyes peeking out. Abbie blew a stray lock of hair from her face and concentrated, her hands held out in front of her as if she were conducting an orchestra.

Nothing happened.

"You're trying too hard, little one," said Nadiene over her shoulder as she pulled some apples from her pack.

"Not trying hard enough," wagered Charles, snagging the piece of fruit his companion tossed to him.

"Shhh," hissed Foster.

Abbie took a deep breath and closed her eyes, standing still for a long moment. She'd done this before, but doing it *again* was proving to be more difficult. Opening one eye, Abbie peeked at the others, catching sight of Gwyn a short way off talking to Bryn, the ice troll. She quickly scrunched her eyes shut again before Foster could tell her to.

Air was all around her. She was *breathing* the air. There was a breeze ruffling the fur of her hood. No big deal. Abbie quirked her fingers and then gestured as if she were commanding the violins to begin the first movement, her eyes fluttering. She could *almost* see the air around her moving, and she quickly *pushed* at it. The breeze whooshed past her, and her eyes flew open.

"I did it!"

Foster's hood had blown back, his blond curls in disarray. "You did!" He grinned and punched his fist toward her. She tapped it with her own, "blowing" it up with style. The elf slowly opened his own hand, and she giggled.

"Break's over," said Gwyn, rejoining the group. "The pass is difficult, but this time of year is the best for using it. During Winter's height it would be impossible."

Abbie looked up at the jagged, snow-covered peaks that loomed ahead of them.

"It still looks impossible."

She flexed her fingers a bit, wondering if she could use her new ability to blow snow off the path.

"Bryn will break the path for us," said Gwyn, gesturing toward the troll who sat like a lump of ice near some trees. "There is, of course, an easier road, but it is the one everyone uses, which is why we are here."

Foster pulled his hood back up, tucking his wild hair into it.

"How do we get back?"

"Back?" Gwyn raised an eyebrow.

"Yes, back. Once we have used the Gate and sent Abbie home?" He scratched his hairline under the hood. "I must get back."

"Yeah," said Abbie, suddenly wondering the same thing. "You guys will make sure Foster gets back to Summer, right?"

"Of course," boomed Charles, putting an arm around the boy and squashing him against his side. "I'm not planning on staying in Winter. Foster will go back with us."

"Yes, yes, it is all settled," said Gwyn impatiently. "Can we move? The longer we stay in one area, the easier it will be for someone to spot us."

Everyone shouldered their packs and fell into place in the line. After a few days in Winter, they had fallen into a new routine much like their patterns in Summer, just with a few differences. They chose campsites differently, prioritized making fires, and felt the presence of the humongous ice troll always lurking nearby. Thanks to gifts from Pan's Lost Children, the temperature was not too much of an issue. Abbie was still cold, of course, but she never thought that she was going to freeze to death.

Big, fluffy snowflakes fell as the path under their feet tilted upward. Bryn's large, flat feet were perfect for packing down the snow so the others could walk on it, though he wasn't winning any points for stealth. If it wasn't for Gwyn continually using his magic to smooth out the snow behind them, there would have been a groove stamped into the snow marking their trail for miles.

Abbie held out a hand while she walked, trying to catch snowflakes on her glove. The thick, wet flakes piled up easily, and she scooped up a handful from the ground, packing it into a snowball. The more she worked at it, the harder and smoother the ball got. She kept packing until she was sure it was too hard to safely throw at anyone.

She grinned impishly and tossed it anyway, nailing Foster in the back. He yelped and fell forward into the snow, even though she hadn't thrown it very hard, and for a moment Abbie panicked and thought she'd hurt him.

When he sat up, however, he had his own snowball and *really* good aim. Abbie couldn't duck in time and caught a mouthful of snow. Spluttering, she fell to her knees and started scooping up more snow, eager to continue the fight.

Nadiene stepped over her with her long legs, reached down, and pulled her back up.

"We don't have time to play."

Her dark face was stern, and she made a guttural noise in her throat that almost sounded like a genuine wolf's growl, quickly settling the two youngsters down. The farther they got into Winter, the more cross Nadiene seemed to get.

"Sorry," said Abbie, ashamed that she'd needed telling off.

Nadiene tweaked Abbie's nose, trying to show that she wasn't *too* mad at them, and the girl wrinkled it up. Tugging her hood back down on her forehead, the little girl refocused her attention on the troll, mimicking his steps and stomping along the trampled path like a miniature version of Bryn. That only entertained her for a few minutes before she was back to trudging along with everyone else. The wind picked up as if the mountains themselves wanted to blow them back down the ravine.

Everyone kept their heads down, looking at their feet as the snow whipped into their eyes. Before the afternoon was over, the group was caught in a full-blown storm, and they were forced to huddle together, using Bryn as a windbreak. The few trees that grew that high up offered scant protection, but with the big ice troll sandwiched between a couple of them, there was just enough room for everyone to find shelter from the worst of the storm.

Nadiene stared out into the distance, her vulpine face unreadable as the skies darkened around them. There was a smattering of small talk as Charles tried to make conversation, but he quickly gave up. Foster sat miserably between Charles and Abbie, hunched up into a compact ball.

In stark contrast, Gwyn stood upright, the wind whipping his white hair around him as he held on to Bryn's arm. He almost disappeared into the snow as it swirled, and Abbie supposed he was keeping watch. She clamped her hands down on her hood to keep it on but caught sight of Foster's miserable face pressed against his knees.

She put her arms around him, pressing her face into the back of his neck in a warm-hearted, childish hug.

"It'll be okay," she said, not sure if he could hear her over the roar of the blizzard.

Foster was trembling, but as she snuggled close to him the elf boy began to relax. Then the sky ripped apart in a thunderous boom that rattled the mountainside.

Both children jumped, terrified. Abbie squeezed her eyes shut and told herself: *There is no storm, no danger. We're okay. I'm back home.* As she thought this, she clung tightly to Foster. The thunder rolled around them, but soon the sounds of the storm faded as the wind died down.

Charles poked Abbie in the back, and she cautiously lifted her head. He pointed up, and she followed his finger with her eyes. The snow drifted lazily around them like the soft fluff inside a snow globe. A dome of some kind had surrounded them with the storm still blowing on the other side.

Inside the dome it was relatively quiet. Abbie's mouth fell open as she looked around, and even Foster raised his head.

"What have you done?" snapped Gwyn, raising his arm until his hand penetrated the ceiling. "Using magic this close to the center of Winter will draw attention." He withdrew his arm, but the dome remained intact.

"It's better than freezing our arses off," said Charles roughly, sitting up straight. He looked down at Abbie and shrugged. "Sorry. I don't know how you're doing it, but please don't stop."

She stood up, cupping her hand under a floating snow-flake, gently lifting until it lay in her hand.

"Did I do this?"

"Instinctively," said Nadiene, glaring at Gwyn until he subsided. "You've generated a protective ward of Air."

Bryn rumbled, but didn't move, and the Winter elf sighed.

"You have got to be more careful," Gwyn said finally. "It is a clever trick but... just be careful!" He shook his head at Abbie and sat down at the edge of the ward.

Foster slowly unraveled his body from the ball he'd been pressed into, looking cautiously around. His eyes looked haunted. To Abbie, he seemed scared and tired, but a tentative smile began to form on his lips.

"A ward is a protective spell," he whispered to her as the grownups snipped at each other.

Charles began digging food out of his bag.

"Once a ward is set, it will last for—well, hours or years. It depends on the amount of magic channeled into it. Look," he said, pointing with just his finger from where his hand was still clutching at his knee. "If you close your eyes halfway, unfocus them a bit, you should be able to see the ward. Little glimmering symbol at the apex of the dome. See it?"

Abbie did as instructed, her eyes nearly crossing as she tried to relax them just right. A squiggly set of lines appeared, surrounded by a circle.

"How did I make that if I don't know what I'm doing?"

"I do not know," Foster replied, resting his head on his knees and closing his eyes. "I do not know any half-elves, nor what they might be capable of. Of course," he added, "I suppose if Gwyn is telling the truth, then your father was a very powerful elf."

Abbie frowned, her thoughts hard to put in order. "He's just my dad. I... I don't know if he is or isn't."

Outside the ward, the wind still howled, but it was much quieter inside the protective dome. Abbie edged closer to Foster until their heads were nearly touching.

"What do you mean, if Gwyn is telling the truth?"

Foster's eyes tracked past her to where the Winter elf sat against Bryn's foot, and then up and behind them to the ice troll they leaned on.

"I did not mean anything by it. Just that... he seems to know your father. Are you not curious to hear what else Gwyn might say about him?"

Abbie frowned lightly. "I guess."

Dad was just Dad to her still. She couldn't quite wrap her eight-year-old brain around the fact that her father had had a life before she was born, let alone that he might have been someone completely different than the teasing, gentle man she knew so well. Foster was right, though. She would have to talk to Gwyn about it before they reached their destination and she went home.

She could almost feel how close they were: perhaps home was just over the next hill, or the one after that one. The weight of her journey settled over her as she anticipated the coming end.

Abbie leaned back against Bryn Bach, who somehow was not as cold as his ice-covered form looked, and touched her face where she'd been bathed in the green-black blood of a goblin back in the Steelwood. *Was that a week ago? Two weeks?* She hadn't been keeping track of the days. A momentary panic seized her chest. How long had she been in the Otherworld? Abbie looked out toward her companions and took some deep breaths, slowly releasing the air in her lungs until her heart stopped thumping so loudly.

She was among friends. Wasn't she?

The little group had spent the night under the ward Abbie had haphazardly created. By morning, the storm was over, so Gwyn showed her how she could dismiss the ward and leave no magical trace that they had been there. She "blew" the ward away, the symbol dissolving.

Nadiene rubbed the bridge of her hawkish nose and helped Abbie put her pack on. The thieftaker seemed quieter lately, though it was hard to tell if that was just because of where they were. Winter affected all of them differently.

Gwyn, of course, seemed unchanged. Foster trudged forward with his head down, his hood obscuring his face as he concentrated on putting one foot in front of the other. Charles was less boisterous than he had been, but he always had a ready smile and a wink for Abbie whenever she looked back.

Nadiene barely spoke unless she was spoken to. As they walked through the mountain pass, she constantly looked around, and Abbie could see the woman's nostrils flaring as she smelled the air. Sometimes at night, if the stars were bright or they had managed to make a fire, the girl saw Nadiene looking at a piece of paper. She'd never managed to get a close look, but that night she mentioned it to Foster. Without hesitation, he abruptly stood up and sat next to the wolf as she looked at the paper in question.

"What is that?"

Nadiene folded it away immediately, glaring at him. "Nothing."

"You have been looking at it for the last few nights," he said, taking Abbie completely at her word without a question. "So what is it? A plan to get into the Palace?"

"It is noth—" She paused. "Yes, it has to do with the Winter Palace. Now go away."

His sharp eyes had caught a word or two on the paper before she had secreted it away, words inscribed around what had appeared to be a drawing of a building.

"Wolfsbane?"

Nadiene's face tightened, and Charles made a low, rumbling noise as he focused on their conversation from across the tiny fire. "It is nothing. I swear," she said.

"Wolfsbane Scepter, perhaps?" said Gwyn, suddenly interested, and Nadiene's amber eyes glowed as they settled on him.

"That is not real," dismissed Foster. "Is it?"

"What's a… Wolfsbane Scepter?" asked Abbie while Nadiene glowered.

"A powerful Forest artifact," said Gwyn. "Created in Summer by the Queen there." He looked at the wolf with renewed interest, almost as if he'd never really bothered to look at her before. "It was used to bind wolfkind to the elven royals."

Nadiene flushed, her dark skin burnished bronze in the firelight. "I know it is at the heart of Winter, in that Queen's possession. Once I have it, I can break the hold they have over my people."

"Really?" asked Abbie, wide-eyed.

"Yes," said Nadiene, focusing on the girl. "The Pack is enslaved to the Queens and their lords and ladies. Always doing their bidding." The gold of her eyes intensified, and Abbie awkwardly looked away before meeting them again. "I left the Pack, but if the call from the Queen is strong enough, it would catch me up again."

"Leaving the Pack is like deciding to cut off your own arm," supplied Charles helpfully. "None do it lightly, and practically no one does it at all."

"Is that why you pledged to bring Abbie to Winter's heart?" asked Gwyn. "Just so you could have your chance at the Scepter?"

Abbie sat up straighter while Nadiene suddenly stuttered. "N-no, of course not. I mean, *yes*, it was a consideration..."

Charles sighed. "I know how important this is to you, Nadi, but—"

"I won't get another shot at this," she retorted. "Of course, we get Abbie home first. That has always been the plan."

"And if you find an opportunity to go for the Scepter *before* that happens?" Gwyn shook his head. "You might ruin her only chance to go home, to chase this fantasy."

"It isn't like that, I promise," Nadiene said, looking pointedly at Abbie again. The girl squirmed, feeling very uncomfortable. "But once she is safely through the Gate, why do you care what I do?"

"Once we use the Gate, all of Winter will be alerted to our presence," replied Gwyn. "You will have little to no time for searching the Palace. It is far too large for a simple search. Believe me, I know."

"I have a map," she said. "I have been memorizing it." Nadiene pulled the paper back out, unfolding it and letting Gwyn see it clearly. "The Wolfsbane Scepter is in the—"

He waved a hand dismissively. "And how did you get that in Summer? No one there knows what the Palace looks like. You are lucky I came along, or you would be in the dungeons before you ever set foot in the Gateroom."

"The map is accurate," she said grimly.

"You will be distracted when we arrive, which will put us all in danger," Gwyn said, his icy blue eyes glittering. "You started this trip under false pretenses—I suppose your human here had already told you no?"

Charles shifted. "I knew you had this thought in your head, Nadiene, but still, even now?" He shook his head. "Gwyn is right; this is a distraction we can't afford."

Nadiene folded the map and clutched it tightly in her hand before stuffing it back into her pack. "My word is my word." The wolf looked at Abbie. "I swear on the moon I will see you home."

"You cannot trust her," said Gwyn indignantly. "She lied to you about why she wanted to go to Winter!"

Foster looked concerned as the older people threw words back and forth, and he edged back to Abbie's side.

"What do you think?" he asked.

"I don't know." She watched the others with wide eyes. Why did grownups have to be so confusing? Abbie didn't really like confrontations, and she didn't like how Gwyn and Nadiene were suddenly arguing over her like she wasn't even there.

"She trusts me," Nadiene said, standing now, facing Gwyn. "Don't you, Abbie? I'm going to see this through. You know this."

"My bond to Abbie is deeper than an accidental meeting," the Winter elf said sharply. "Her father, Wodan, and I—"

"Oh, stuff it about her father. I'm talking to *you*, Abbie." Nadiene stepped closer to the girl, kneeling in front of her. "You know I am speaking the truth." She looked ragged, her features more wolfish than normal, and when she held out a hand, Abbie flinched. Nadiene pretended not to notice, leaving her hand out and empty until the girl tentatively took it. She held firmly but gently, adding, "I will see you to the Gate in Winter, as I pledged before."

"She will use you and the others as a distraction and go after her real prize," interjected Gwyn. "You should send her away."

Abbie's eyes grew even bigger, and she held on to the woman's hand.

"Send her away?"

"It is your choice, of course," said Gwyn. "I will not guide her to the Palace, not if she is going to rob my Queen." He crossed his arms firmly, his handsome face setting grimly.

Nadiene's eyes tracked back from Gwyn to Abbie, and she squeezed her hand once before releasing her.

"I can get us there on my own."

"I would not wager on it," he said. "Abbie, you must decide who will take you to the Gate. Me, with my first-hand knowledge, or this woman who has deceived you."

The girl felt the weight of the choice she'd been asked to make; it was a great, heavy decision with edges she couldn't quite grasp. "I... I don't know?" She looked at Charles, whose mouth was set into a firm line behind his beard.

Abbie turned to Foster, who was studying the wolf from where he sat. "What do you think?"

The elven boy's mouth twisted into a grimace, and he shrugged under his warm clothes.

"Wolves will always look out for themselves," he said. Nadiene's face darkened and she opened her mouth, but he hurried on. "That is what I have always been told. You are the first I have ever truly met, and I do like you." His eyes met Abbie's, and she could see fear growing in them. "We will probably have just one chance to get you through the Gate and back home."

She clutched at his hand, desperate for some connection as Nadiene and Gwyn glared at each other over her head. As the moments dragged on and she still didn't say anything, Charles got to his feet and stood between them.

"Give her a minute," he said roughly, putting his hands out toward Gwyn but stopping short of touching him. Nadiene met her partner's eyes and sighed, stepping back and kneeling at her pack.

Gwyn smirked. "Abbie is lucky to have such a loyal pet." He retreated to where Bryn Bach was lurking.

The bearded thieftaker turned to the two children, crouching down in the snow to be on their level. "Seems we're at a crossroads." He looked into Abbie's eyes, and she stared back, her face a mask of confusion. "Nadiene won't travel with Gwyn. And he won't with her. I promised I'd keep you safe and see you home, and that hasn't changed, as far as I'm concerned."

He didn't offer any opinions, but Abbie guessed he supported Nadiene, seeing as they had been partners long before she had come along.

"Do I have to choose?" she asked in a small voice.

"I can't make the decision for you, little one," Charles said. "Nadiene will take you there; I know her word is good. But we're in the middle of Winter with a Winter elf." He looked over his shoulder at Gwyn, and then back, trying to infuse the glance with a meaning that Abbie couldn't pick up on.

She huddled with Foster, talking quietly for a few minutes as snow began to fall gently around them. When she stood up, she felt ready—until Gwyn and Nadiene both looked at her expectantly.

"I, uh, know what we have to do." Abbie licked her lips and regretted it in the bitter cold that nipped at her face. She took a deep breath and dragged her eyes over to the wolf. "I'm sorry, Nadiene."

CHAPTER 16

Changeling

FIONA WAS FADING away under the influence of the changeling. Dan watched his wife brush her teeth as she got ready for bed, smiling when she caught him in the mirror. She finished up her nightly ablutions, crawling into bed beside him with bone-deep weariness.

He helped her pull the comforter up to her chin the way she liked it, brushing her long hair out of her face.

"Why so serious?" she asked sleepily, her eyes already closing.

"Just thinking about how much I love you," Dan said, lying on top of the covers next to her and taking her hand. Her skin was soft, and the bones underneath seemed frail, like a bird's.

"I love you, too." She yawned, snuggling into her pillow.

The image of the pond superimposed itself over the bedroom in his mind, not as it was, but how it must have been—green and full of life. The changeling clawed its way out of the water, its touch shriveling the grass as it struggled for life. Death spread out from it as it lay on the bank in the dying ferns, draining the area of energy.

Fiona squeezed his hand, startling him out of his daydream. He smiled down at her, unable to get out of his head the image of the changeling sucking her life force away.

"Whatever it is that's bothering you," she murmured, "it's going to be okay."

He laughed, trying to choke back a sudden surge of emotion as she comforted him. "I hope so."

Dan leaned forward and kissed her forehead and then her lips as she tilted her face toward him.

The changeling would kill her.

Was Abbie's life worth losing Fiona?

He could barely touch the elemental magic of the Otherworld while in this one. But he had been sent through to exile with a disguise placed upon him. An illusion of Air spun by the Queen herself as she banished the Hunt.

Dan closed his eyes, pulling at the illusion with all his might, unraveling it and then absorbing the energy before it could slip away. He kissed his wife as she drifted off to sleep, the magical energy turning into light and settling on her skin.

Fiona breathed deeply, already fast asleep. He could feel the light inside her, already giving her some strength. With a sigh, he pushed up from the bed, careful not to jostle her. In the cocoon of the bed, only her head showed, her blond hair fanning out on the pillow.

He walked to the bathroom and looked in the mirror, turning his head and peering at his ears. The cartilage stretched up into delicate points. His face, too, had changed—a harder, more angular look to his cheekbones. An arched brow seemed haughty, rather than curious.

This was the Horned One, the leader of the Wild Hunt. Wodan gazed at himself, then past his reflection to Fiona sleeping in their bed. It would happen soon. He would return to the Otherworld to retrieve Abbie, despite the death sentence set on him should he ever return.

He stalked out of the bedroom and down the stairs to the kitchen.

The changeling stood in the living room eyeballing Sammy who cowered in his bed.

"You don't remember him, do you?" he asked.

It looked up at him, brown eyes widening at his appearance. "I do not," it said. "It is a useless creature."

"Leave Fiona alone."

"I cannot." It looked up, as if it could see through the ceiling and into their bedroom. "I must live."

"You are alive—you do not need more from her."

"Sacrifice is needed."

"I am Wodan of the Wild Hunt." He drew himself up to his full height, glaring down at the small changeling. "You will obey me."

Its eyes tracked to his, and it put its hands on its hips in a very Abbie-like gesture that broke his heart and enraged him at the same time. "You have no power here, elf."

Wodan took a step forward, to pick it up or throttle it he wasn't sure, and the changeling thrust its palm out, eyes flashing bright green as a terrible energy shoved Wodan back. His feet slid on the hardwood, but he kept his balance as his anger threatened to boil over. Any energy the changeling spent was energy it would have to recoup from Fiona until it had drained her dry. Wodan took a breath, putting his hands up, palms out in a placating gesture.

"Be calm."

"Be gone!" The changeling shouted at him, Abbie's face distorted with rage. It moved toward him, and he took a step back, unwilling to hurt it. He still needed it to rescue Abbie.

A smile curled across the little girl's face at his retreat. "Leave me alone, elf. You cannot command me or stop me." It paused. "If you leave, I will spare her life."

"A lie," Wodan eyed it uneasily. He could lock it in a closet until the Cat was ready. But what if it expended all its energy trying to escape and then died?

"A Deal," it said, the hard edges of the word emphasized.

"I leave you with Fiona? Never."

The changeling sat on the edge of the coffee table in Abbie's nightgown, toes brushing the rug. "I am a child. I need a parent. If you are gone, she is necessary. She may be weakened, but she will live. A Bargain can be struck," it said, the words weighty with promised power.

Wodan thought carefully. "I will leave you with her, and you keep her alive?"

"Yes. Unless you return."

"We have a Deal," he said. "I will leave, and you spare Fiona's life."

"Done." A tingle raised gooseflesh on his skin as the Bargain magic settled upon them. Once he left the house, the changeling would be forced to keep Fiona alive—unable to harm her further.

Wodan didn't stop to pack a bag; he just walked out the front door.

He would return.

CHAPTER 17

Ice Palace

THE DAYS SINCE they had parted from the wolf had passed quietly. Charles had been quiet, and Foster a little more on edge. Gwyn was the only companion able to muster up a smile. He seemed friendlier, more relaxed.

Abbie found it very strange to make camp without Nadiene's sharp eyes taking everything in, and losing her helping hands had shifted more work on to the two children. Still, by the second night, they had a new routine, even if the Nadiene-shaped hole in the group still tugged at them. Abbie felt that she had betrayed the older woman, though Gwyn assured her it was the opposite.

Traveling down the other side of the mountain was easier than the hike up—even the snow wasn't quite as deep—and Abbie found herself free to enjoy more of her surroundings. While Summer had been awash in color, Winter seemed monochromatic until you really *looked*.

The trees on this side of the mountain pass were various shades of evergreen. Snow and ice coated their branches, with one grove of trees completely covered in icicles sparkling in the sun. Snowdrops grew through the snow in places, their light green stems standing out against the white fields. Foster picked one, placing it almost reverently in his pack.

Abbie watched him close his pack, then she flopped over backward into the snow.

"Are you okay?" blurted Foster, struggling over to her and looking down as she swept her arms and legs back and forth wildly over the snow.

"Yes!" she breathed, doing a few more passes with her limbs for good measure before sitting up and jumping free of her mark.

"What are you doing?" the Summer elf asked, baffled.

"Snow angels!" Abbie fell over again to make another one, flailing in the soft snow. Foster laughed at the absurdity of it all.

"It does not look—" he started, then Abbie interrupted.

"Here's the dress and the wings," she pointed. The elf twisted his head this way and that, and she sighed, wiggling to get all the snow off her backside. Charles brushed her off and helped her readjust the cloak that she should have been wearing, chuckling at her snow angel when she pointed it out.

"What is going on?" asked Gwyn. "Never mind, please do not tell me." He brushed aside the tree boughs in front of him. "We are here."

Abbie peered through the opening excitedly, then she giggled at the troll blocking the view. "We're at Bryn's butt?"

"What? Oh." Gwyn pushed on the ice troll, grumbling at him to get out of the way. "Never mind that. The Heart of Winter, the Palace, the seat of the Queen of Air and Darkness." He sketched out a little bow, his long hair falling forward.

Foster and Abbie crowded forward, and she gasped as she looked down into the valley. A great castle sat in the valley before them. It looked as if it was made entirely of upside-down icicles glistening in the late afternoon sun. White spires reached for the pale blue sky, but the sunlight seemed to refract into pink, lavender, blue, and green as it touched the milky stones.

The vast distance and all evergreens that surrounded it still obscured most of the castle. Foster plucked at Gwyn's sleeve, his breath fogging around his head.

"How are we going to get past all those trees?"

"I was thinking you could do something about that, Guardian," said the Winter elf.

The boy looked back down toward the Palace, studying the area they would have to walk through.

"Dusk would be the best time," he said slowly. "Neither night, nor day—the trees are sleepiest then." Foster looked up at Gwyn and Charles. "What about the inside of the Palace?"

The two adults were quiet for a little bit. Abbie watched them carefully as they exchanged glances. The Gate being inside the heart of Winter was all well and good, but now that they were here, she wasn't sure there was any plan beyond "get inside and through the Gate."

"Are there guards?" she asked.

"Yes," replied Gwyn. "There are minimal guards—we do not exactly hibernate through Summer's height, but the lords and ladies spend the time in their own estates. Usually," he added, but with a smile that put Abbie at ease.

Charles's hand was on his leather-wrapped sword hilt.

"We will sneak in until we can't, then we'll fight."

He looked grim and determined, and the contrast between him and Gwyn was vaguely upsetting, but Abbie couldn't put into words why.

She took Foster's hand, finding comfort in his presence.

"We have a few hours to wait," said the elven boy, looking at her with kind eyes and giving her hand a squeeze. "And then you will be home."

Abbie smiled, daring to believe it would be true.

They spent the hours before they were to walk down into the valley resting and planning. Gwyn gave Charles his cloak, so with the hood pulled up he could pass as a Winter elf—except for his big red beard, which the human adamantly refused to cut.

"I'm not freezing my chin off for this. Even if I did, it would only take one look under the hood for an elf to realize I'm not one of them."

He did allow Abbie to braid it, however, and she tied it off into three small plaits, concentrating on her task while he snoozed.

Abbie scooped snow into piles, packing them together in a rough approximation of a snowman. Broken twigs from the recent storm served for arms and a bit of nose.

"You must make sure you do not use your Air magic by accident," said Foster, watching her play. He drew glyphs in the snow in front of him with a stick. "Beyond what I use to sneak us through the guardian trees, we will need to be very quiet."

Both children looked up, their eyes drawn to the hulking shape of Bryn Bach. The troll's eyes gleamed blue, and it *harrumphed*, shifting its bulk so they were facing its back.

"A big troll doesn't seem like a very stealthy sort of thing to bring with us," Abbie said.

"Bryn will be coming." Gwyn had been listening in on their conversation. "His presence legitimizes us—the Queen employs trolls to guard the grounds, and many elves do not care to learn how to tell them apart."

He patted Bryn's knee, the icy skin of the troll not bothering him.

"Well, I'm glad," Abbie said, smiling up at the big creature.

Bryn's craggy face split into what one might generously call a smile, then returned to stare ponderously down into the valley.

The time finally arrived, and Foster dubiously pulled at his hair where it had been pulled forward to cover his ears. His hair set him apart from Winter elves, so the idea was that he would be passed off as a human child, along with Abbie, in case any guards stopped them.

Abbie took Foster's hand, giving it a squeeze, and they walked down into the forest together.

Abbie hardly dared breathe as they traveled through the trees. The pines and firs towered above the little group in that quiet moment between sunset and night, and they all seemed affected by the gloomy atmosphere.

Abbie looked sideways under her hood to Foster, who had woven a calming Earth glyph and maintained it as they continued through the forest. Lacking a gift for the earthen element, it wasn't a thing she could *see*, but the trees seemed to sigh and whisper as they walked underneath them. Branches dipped lower and stayed at ease after they passed.

The castle loomed ahead, only visible in glimpses through the trees. *Mom and Dad and home are through there*, thought Abbie. She clenched her hands into fists at her sides. They were going home. In her mind, it was impossible that they might fail.

Charles peered out into the woods, nearly halting the entire group before he continued walking forward. When Gwyn looked at him, he shrugged as he ducked under a low branch. Abbie glanced around, a prickle between her shoulder blades. *Was that movement between the trees?* She rubbed her eyes and stared, but they were surrounded by a sea of tree trunks. Everything in the forest was still and quiet, except for them.

Bryn made his way between the trees in his strange, troll way. Despite his bulk and height, the ice troll seemed to find the perfect openings between the firs and pines where he could slot through without disturbing the drowsy trees. It seemed like magic to Abbie, and perhaps it was.

The group paused at the edge of the forest, a pale aqua and white wall erupting from the ground twenty meters away. Abbie could feel her heart beating in her neck and tried taking deep breaths to calm down.

They waited for what seemed like interminable minutes at the edge of the trees until Bryn, for no reason Abbie could discern, walked out into the open. Gwyn held the rest of them back for a few moments and then nodded.

"The way is clear."

Abbie's breath fogged around her head as she stepped away from the forest, the sky deepening to a dark navy above her. She looked up as they moved toward the Palace walls. The stars twinkled in the cloudless sky as she focused on the building they approached.

The walls were smooth and lit with blue-white torches every few yards, alternating at ground level and along the top where, presumably, guards were walking. The group quickly covered the area between the forest and the castle, disappearing into its shadow as Abbie realized there was a door in front of them. It was large enough for Bryn to squeeze through, but she had to look down at her toes with "proper reverence" as a pair of Winter elves stopped them.

"State your business," one said, her voice hard.

"Bringing these two children in from the cold," said Gwyn easily. Charles stood where the troll partially blocked the guards' view of him. "Is that any way to greet a lord of Winter?" Gwyn added with a bit of edge.

"Runaways?" she asked.

Gwyn nodded. "Just so. If we may...?" He gestured toward the double doors—the southern gate into the Palace grounds.

The guard stepped aside, her partner doing the same, and Gwyn strode through the doors, the children following him dutifully. Abbie peeked at Foster, and he met her eyes from under his hood. She couldn't help but feel excited about where they were, and it showed on her face. He, on the other hand, looked ill.

"Are you okay?" she whispered.

"Yes," he said. Then, "No. I—"

"You can look up now," said Gwyn quietly. "There aren't many soldiers wandering about, and the wolves are mostly outside the walls."

"Mostly?" asked Charles.

Abbie gasped. Magnificent ice sculptures of flowers and trees surrounded them. Some were larger than life, and others looked so delicately real they seemed impossible. Paths wove throughout the courtyard, lit with more cold fire torches. Gwyn herded the children through, while Bryn traveled around the edge where he wouldn't step on anything fragile.

"The Ice Gardens," Gwyn said hurriedly. "Quickly now."

Abbie looked up one last time at the foreign stars before Gwyn hustled them into the Palace proper. It was only marginally warmer inside, and Abbie almost immediately slipped on the smooth stone floor. Charles grabbed her arm to steady her.

The path they took through the Palace involved many twists and turns. At times, Abbie was certain she could hear footsteps behind them, but it appeared to be echoes of their own feet as Gwyn kept them moving as fast as he could. Foster's tanned face was pale under his hood, and she tried to imagine how scary this was for him.

Logically, Abbie knew she should be afraid as well—after all, her companions had talked up how terrible and frightening the Queens were since she'd set foot in the Otherworld. Instead, a sense of excitement surged through her. *Going home, going home*, she thought with each step, nearly skipping. Days and days had passed since getting here. Weeks, perhaps. And now, it seemed, her journey was coming to its end.

"The throne room is ahead," said Gwyn. The group slowed and stopped, waiting for him to lead them forward.

"No guards?" Charles eyed the massive hallway they had to cross to reach the double doors. They were ornately carved with seasonal iconography and inlaid with massive amounts of silver and mother-of-pearl. "Is *She* in there?" he asked the Winter elf.

"Not exactly," said Gwyn.

Abbie could barely stand the thought of waiting another minute. "Come on then," she said, and ran across the empty hallway to the huge doors.

"Wait!" called Charles, and she could hear him running after her as she reached the entrance to the throne room.

She put her hands on the doors and pulled, and a blast of cold air and snow swirled out of the room, enveloping her.

CHAPTER 18

The Furious Host

WODAN, LORD OF the Wild Hunt, the Horned One, Fae Prince, and scapegoat, stood in the woods behind his house. He'd retrieved items long hidden, remnants of his previous life. He strapped the silvered sword and bronze daggers to his belt and carefully unwrapped the Horn of the Great Hunt, made from a tusk of the ancient Twrch Trwyth, the Great Boar.

Wodan put out the Call, blowing the Horn to call up the Hunt. The sound was immense, a keening blast that was felt as much as heard. The Hunters would not fail to hear its magical call, no matter where they might be.

He waited.

As night fell on the third day, the first arrived, drawn by instincts they could not resist. Harry and his hound walked out of the trees into the clearing, his eyes immediately drawn to the circle of death surrounding the pond. Others followed; all Fae hunters of Summer who had been bound to the Hunt for thousands of years. They wore human faces and forms, and most looked surprised to find Wodan before them with his disguise stripped away. He stood stoically as they gathered, the music of insects the only sound as the clearing filled.

The Winter Hunters did not come. His fellow leader, Gwyn app Nudd, could have called and commanded them. Wodan put thoughts of the son of Nudd aside, to be dealt with later.

Mathan arrived last, the werebear in human form, broad-shouldered and ill-tempered. Even he knew better than to say anything.

"I have called up the Hunt to protect the balance between the Seasons." A murmur followed Wodan's words, which he ignored. "We were discarded, but there is still a job to do."

"There is no Boar to chase," said Enid, a tall female elf with a tawny blond mane of hair. She wore a T-shirt, jeans, and a no-nonsense attitude. "We were cast to this world to preserve the Bargain between seasons."

"The world changes around us," he continued, as if she had not spoken. "Something, or someone, has found a loophole in the Bargain. A changeling has come—"

"This is just about your daughter," interrupted Mathan, his words a low growl.

"What about his daughter?" asked another Hunter, as Enid said, "What daughter?"

"She was taken to the Otherworld." Harry knelt beside his hound and ran his hand over the dog's sleek fur. "I take it she was found?"

"Yes. As far as I know she is still alive and free." Wodan drew himself up to his full height. "I need your help to take the changeling alive—and use it to open a portal back home."

The Hunters looked at each other in the moonlight. "What if we wish to have no part in this?" asked Harold.

"I cannot force you to do anything," Wodan replied, hiding his disappointment. "I must try, regardless. Yet all who help—you may use the portal."

"And break the Bargain?" Enid was aghast.

"We made no Deal," pointed out Mathan, intrigued. "We were pawns in the long game the Queens must play."

"We remain here until they must call the Hunt once more," interjected Brandon, a wolf. He ran his hands through his shaggy brown hair. "They must call it up again. Someday."

"If we go through, who knows what might happen between the Seasons?" Enid gestured around the moonlit clearing. "Only our Summer brothers and sisters are here. With Gwyn app Nudd absent—"

"He lives and is already on the other side." Wodan looked at the hunters as they fell silent. "If the rules do not apply to him, they do not apply to us."

"He has been in the Otherworld this *whole time?*" roared Mathan. "While we rot in this human-infested—"

"*Regardless,*" said Wodan loudly. "I need the changeling. Without harm coming to the human inside the house. If you follow me, you follow me; if you leave—do not return next time you hear the Horn."

"The Hound has not yet jumped down," said Harold mildly, his dog appearing larger as it looked up at him. "I follow the Wild Hunt." He had once been a human king of the Britons but running with the Hunters had prolonged his life unnaturally. Wodan inclined his head in acknowledgment of the man's pledge.

One by one, the other Hunters pledged, the hope of returning home flickering to life in their eyes. Mathan came last. "I follow Wodan and the Wild Hunt," he said. He glanced at the dead grass under their feet. "I take it this is where it came through?"

Wodan nodded. "For now, it is gathering its strength in my house."

The bear lifted his head, scenting the air through flared nostrils. "It smells like death here," he said, stating the obvious. "What is your plan?"

"The changeling pressed me into a Deal," Wodan said. "It will leave my wife alive, as long as I do not return to the house." He locked eyes with Mathan. "Which is why you will capture it."

Mathan snorted, but there was no scorn in his voice. "And the Cat?"

"What about the Cat?" asked Enid, close enough to overhear. "That dragonkind cannot be trusted."

"Can any dragon? He contacted the Cat about his child," the bear said blandly, and they both stared at Wodan. "Well?"

He did not like the skepticism of the Hunters, so soon after repledging their loyalty. He raised an eyebrow, but knew he must answer. "The Cat located Abbie for me, in exchange for access to the portal the changeling will open for us."

Enid gave him a long look and then nodded. "A fair enough Bargain." She tossed her hair back, looking up at Mathan. "Come, we will get the changeling, with Bran and—" she named three more of the Hunt. They split from the main group, leaving about ten Hunters in the woods.

"The rest of us will guard the portal site," Wodan pointed to the far side of the pond. He didn't have to say *in case the Cat betrays us*. Harry and his hound circled the water in the other direction, while the Hunt spread into the trees.

Wodan stood beside the toadstool circle, the white caps of the fungi bright in the moonlight. A rangy wolf padded into the clearing, its brown fur blending in with the dark ground beneath the pines. After a moment of staring, it shook itself, fur receding into skin as it changed into its human form.

"Do you have the changeling?" the wolf asked, unconcerned about his nakedness as he addressed Wodan.

"Are you the Cat's associate?" Wodan countered.

"I am." The wolf looked around, his brown hair shaggy and growing thickly down his neck, across his shoulders and upper back. "The changeling?"

"Soon." Wodan maintained eye contact with the wolf.

The other looked away lazily, unconcerned about any shows of dominance, but he showed his teeth in a smile. "We will proceed as soon as you hold up your end of the Bargain."

"Consider it upheld," said Enid, melting out of the woods behind the wolf, who turned slowly to face her. Mathan bent through the low-hanging branches of the trees, the changeling slung over his back.

Its hands and elbows were tied together, and it was gagged to prevent it from calling up any more magic. Wodan steeled his expression; the sight of something that looked like his daughter bound and captive was breaking his heart. She could be in a similar situation on the other side of the portal.

"No trouble taking it?" he asked, and Enid shrugged. "My wife?"

"She was not harmed further," said Mathan.

"Shall we?" Wodan asked the wolf, as Mathan dropped the changeling roughly to the ground near the circle. The bear curled his lip at the Cat's associate as he passed him, the changeling wiggling against its bonds in front of Wodan.

"Just a moment," said the wolf. He pressed a finger to his ear and added, "They're ready."

"Who's ready?" Wodan frowned.

"You are, finally," called a familiar female voice. Green eyes shone in the shadows of the trees, and the Cat slunk into view. She stretched languidly, pulling her arms straight over her head before rolling her neck, unconcerned by the gathering of Hunters, who were wary of the dragon—even in human form she was a formidable opponent.

"I have to admit, I did not expect you to bring so many witnesses to our little *tête à tête.*" The Cat stepped over the changeling and lifted her hand as though she was going to touch Wodan's cheek but stopped just short. "Your face has slipped, Wodan." A smile spread across hers. "I like it."

He squared his shoulders. "Is Abbie still alive?"

The Cat looked away, miffed that he ignored her advances. "Yes. Though the danger becomes greater every moment."

"Then let us begin." He knelt beside the changeling, whose face was streaked with dirt and tears. "I propose a new Bargain, creature."

Its eyes sparkled green as it glared at him, but it nodded.

"I will release you, and you will not fight back against me, my companions, or my daughter. You will open a portal to the Otherworld, the size and duration of my choosing. After this is complete, you will have your freedom—on the other side."

The changeling closed its eyes, nodding after a long moment. The Cat looked down curiously, her high heels sinking slightly into the soft earth. Wodan loosened the changeling's gag. "The Deal is struck," it said, and he repeated the words, the magic binding them to the agreement tingling against his skin.

He cut the creature's bonds, and it sat up, rubbing its wrists. Mathan grunted with amusement as it gave him a sour look.

Wodan turned to the Cat. "Is your wolf ready?"

She raised an eyebrow. "My wolf?" She regarded the one in question, who responded with a slight shrug. "Oh, no. He is not going with you."

"Then who?" Wodan asked, a little too loudly. "I do not have time for more games. Who is going through with me?"

"I am." The Cat grinned at his expression. "Come now. As you said, no time to waste."

"To where should this portal open?" asked the changeling, Abbie's voice salt in a wound to Wodan's ears. He looked at the Cat, who waggled her eyebrows in reply and bent to the changeling's ear, whispering. She flipped her purple hair out of her eyes as she straightened, her high fashion wildly out of place in the middle of the darkening forest.

"I thought you said you did not make house calls?" Wodan frowned at the thought of taking a dragon through the portal. Couldn't she simply return to the Otherworld when she wished?

"Depends on the house," she said obliquely. "I trust you are ready, Hunter."

He placed his hand on the hilt of his sword, nodding. Around them, the gathered remnants of the Furious Host straightened their stances, standing at the ready. The Cat seemed to ignore their presence.

"Now, please," she said to the changeling, who looked first to Wodan, per their Deal. He nodded.

Abbie's doppelganger focused on the fairy ring, stepping just inside it and raising its small arms toward the center. Energy bubbled up from its torso, a mixture of earth and water elements that wove into a glimmering sigil. It stretched into a roiling circle that rippled and reflected the surrounding forest. Wodan stepped up behind the changeling, his reflection looming in the energy as it widened and grew tall enough even for Mathan to step through. The changeling's eyes rolled up in its head as it concentrated on the gate, and the Cat's lupine associate stepped next to them, holding the creature that looked like a girl upright as it maintained the portal.

The reflection shimmered, and he could see a young elf with curly hair, his back turned to the Gate. It seemed to be a dark room of some kind—the image solidified further and Wodan saw Abbie standing beside the elf, turning toward the portal.

"Wait!" said the Cat, but he could not. Wodan stepped through the Gate to reach his daughter at last.

CHAPTER 19

Grandmother's House

ABBIE'S EYES FILLED with angry tears.

She had opened the throne room that was supposed to house the Gate that would take her home, but instead she faced a wintry forest filled with falling snow. As Charles reached her side, she stamped her foot angrily, one foot on the stone floor of the palace, the other in the snow.

"It's not fair!"

He took in the view, scooping her up into his arms, and she sobbed, her exhaustion suddenly too much to bear.

"We're where we want to be," the burly man reassured her. "Just an elven trick."

Gwyn and Foster joined them, the ice troll bringing up the rear.

"Hurry, hurry," said the Winter elf. "Get inside. We have to close the doors."

He pulled the heavy doors shut, blocking out the sight of the polished stone hallway and leaving a set of doors that seemed to stand in the middle of the forest.

There was an obvious trail through the trees inside the room, but they huddled by the doorway for a moment.

"Bryn will stay here," said Gwyn, "and guard the entrance."

Abbie's lips quivered as Charles put her back on her feet. As she wiped at her tearful face, she felt ashamed of her outburst. She didn't know how to talk about it, so she settled into a sullen silence, staring at her feet.

Charles looked at Gwyn, a guarded look on his face. "You didn't tell me about this."

"I have not been inside for a few cycles," said Gwyn. "She changes the decor from time to time."

"Decor?" said Charles incredulously. He waved an arm at the forest and path, the ceiling disguised by low-hanging clouds still sprinkling snow. Despite the late hour, the 'room' gave the illusion of daylight.

Gwyn didn't answer, walking forward down the path. "She will know we are here. Hurry."

Charles took Abbie's hand while she grabbed Foster's, towing him along as they trudged into the trees.

Abbie couldn't bear the thought of another long journey. *Have we been transported to another place, or is all this forest really inside a room in the palace?* She turned to Foster and saw that he looked as upset as she felt. She squeezed his hand, and he looked at her.

"Are the trees real?" she asked.

"I think so," he said. "I am afraid to use magic to find out."

"Shh," hissed Gwyn. "I can get us through, but *please* be quiet."

Abbie stuck out her tongue to try to make Foster laugh, but he could only manage a faint smile. She felt calmer and more in control again, knowing that she wanted to cheer him up. The path led them through the tall firs, which quickly disappeared into the overhanging fog. Then the trees thinned out, and the group found themselves in a snow-filled clearing.

A cabin sat amid a huddle of pines, a thin curl of smoke rising from its haphazard chimney. Gwyn looked thoughtful as he surveyed the area, and he nodded slowly.

A thick layer of snow blanketed everything, and Charles's beard frosted over with ice crystals as he led the way toward the cabin.

Cheeks reddened from the cold, Abbie pulled at Foster's hand, looking into the green eyes of the Summer elf.

"We made it."

Foster nodded, but said nothing, perfectly miserable as the wind gusted around him and blew powdered snow in his face. Abbie reached over and pulled his cowl tighter around his face, pulling his cloak firmly closed. Snow stuck to his curls.

Walking behind Charles as he broke through the snow, Abbie tried to understand *why* the Queen's throne room might hold a cabin in the woods inside of it. She stumbled, fell face-first into the snow, and came up spluttering. *It seems like just another obstacle in the way of anyone trying to get near the Queen. But maybe she put it here for the fun of it. Or she likes the view?*

Gwyn muttered to himself, but a deafening noise, the sound of cracking ice, sounded from behind. He looked back sharply the way they'd come.

"Hurry, hurry," he said. "We're going to be late."

Charles gripped the handle of his bronze sword, plowing through the knee-deep snow as the children hopped along in his wake. The cabin looked snug, its windows lit with a warm glow as the sky darkened and wind whipped around them. Abbie threw her arm up to protect her face from the stinging ice crystals, and for a moment, the party was stymied as the weather pushed them back.

"Wind," said Gwyn, taking Abbie's shoulder and facing her toward the cabin. She nodded, squinting against the blinding snow, and the Winter elf gave her a shake. "Wind!" he shouted, grabbing her hand and holding it up. "You can stop it!"

Abbie stared at her fingers splayed out in front of her, and then up at the elf. "I can't do it!"

"Yes, you can," he said. "Hurry."

Gwyn looked over his shoulder and gave her a little push forward. The wind roared in her ears, and she gasped as it grew in strength against her.

Abbie swore she could hear wolves howling behind her until the wind tore away all other sound. Shakily, Abbie held both hands out in front of herself, instinctively holding her palms outward in front of her chest as her cloak whipped in the air. She could sense the edges of the wind, feel the currents as they flowed around her, and she held on to the power growing within her.

Thrusting her hands out, she pulled the wind apart, using the air against itself to create calm within the storm. She could simply *feel* how to do it; there was no other way to describe it. Abbie turned, about to say something excitedly to her friends about her success, but they were distracted, all staring toward the rapidly darkening forest. White shapes moved in the trees, seemingly part of the snow itself, until one stopped and howled.

Abbie pulled on Gwyn's arm and he grinned in relief, tapping Charles on the shoulder.

"Quickly!"

Foster ran through the momentary calm Abbie had created, not sparing the false woods behind them another look as more wolves appeared among the trunks. Gwyn ducked through, and Charles backed into the space, his eyes on the trees. Abbie peered out from around him, catching sight of a darker shape slinking behind the white wolves before he continued through the calm, pulling her with him.

"Almost there," said Gwyn, his blue eyes bright in the gathering gloom as he stared at the cabin before them.

Abbie released her hold on the wind with a gasp, and the storm that circled the building returned to full strength, kicking up the swirling snow and nearly obscuring the forest on the other side.

Charles squeezed her shoulder. "I'll go first."

Gwyn stepped out of the way, letting the big human put his hand on the door. There were no locks or ornamentation on the plain wood, and he lifted the latch slowly, pushing the door inward.

Abbie pressed in behind him, eager to see what the room that held the portal to home looked like. It was disappointingly small and dark, lit mostly by a fireplace that burned with ordinary red-orange flames. The chair that sat before it was empty. She pulled Foster inside with her. Gwyn closed the door gently, and the sound of the raging wind outside softened to a dull roar.

"Maybe no one is here," said Foster hopefully.

"Very likely," said Gwyn. "But we must find the portal and activate it. Not much time left."

Charles looked at the Winter elf strangely. "What do you mean, 'not much time left'?"

Abbie walked around the room, examining the little table and cupboard by the window. There was a bowl with a couple eggs in it, a wheel of cheese, and a loaf of bread on the counter. Her stomach growled when she looked at the food, and she reached out to take some.

Foster grabbed her wrist before she could break off a piece of bread.

"Do not eat anything here," he warned. "I feel…" he trailed off, looking around, worried.

She stuck her hands under her cloak to keep them from touching anything by accident. "*What* do you feel?"

Foster shook his head, his lips pressed together in a line, refusing to say more. Abbie continued to study the room. The fireplace was made of stones, and a poker hung nearby, as well as another rod she couldn't place. It had a dog's head on the handle and glittered in the firelight but didn't seem to have much purpose.

Gwyn pulled back a thick curtain made of navy wool, revealing a large mirror hung on the wall opposite the fireplace. He reached out hesitantly, and then tapped the glass. Nothing happened.

Charles pulled back another curtain and stepped away quickly. A small bed was set into an alcove, hidden from the rest of the one-room cabin, and there was someone sleeping in it.

"Is… is that who I think it is?" he whispered.

"The Queen," breathed Foster, his eyes wide with fear.

The woman in the bed appeared to be ancient, her long, white hair bundled under a cap, save a few strands that had escaped while she slept. A blue-and-white checked quilt was pulled up to her wrinkled chin, and she breathed slowly and deeply.

"Grandmother Winter," said Gwyn, rather matter-of-factly, his voice loud in the suddenly silent room. "Do not worry; she is not likely to wake up. Not today. The Solstice is tomorrow," he added, as if that explained everything.

"She is at her weakest," said Foster, but he didn't sound as if he believed it. He moved to the farthest side of the cabin from the sleeping Queen.

"Come here," said Gwyn, beckoning the boy over to the mirror. "You already opened one, so this should be easy."

"Me?" squeaked the Summer elf. "Here?"

"You can do it," Abbie said encouragingly. "I know you can."

"Whatever you're going to do, you'd better hurry," said Charles darkly. He pointed out the window. "The wind is dying down."

They could make out the shapes of the wolves prowling about the cabin. Foster turned to the large mirror with a gulp, brushing his fingers through his curly hair. Gwyn watched the boy, his eyes bright and intense, a faint smile on his face.

"I was… just playing around. It should not have worked," Foster whispered to himself, moving his fingers slowly as he spun up elemental Earth magic. "The portal spell… takes more…"

Abbie couldn't see or make sense of everything Foster was doing, but she could make out the edges of it as he wove together a sigil. The symbol glowed faintly as he settled it against the mirror, but nothing else happened. The Summer elf looked slightly deflated as he stepped back. He wouldn't look Abbie in the eye.

Abbie stared at the mirror. "Is it working?" It didn't look like it was, but she was still a beginner when it came to magic. *Maybe it just needs more time?* she thought.

"I did it the same as before," said Foster, pulling at one of his pointed ears. He met her eyes, and as she read the worry on his face, she began to tear up.

Gwyn put his hand out, and a trickle of Water magic filled the center of the symbol Foster had created. The mirror rippled as the two children gawked at him. He smiled, and pointed over their heads to Charles.

"I would not do that if I were you," said Gwyn.

The big man stopped moving, his hand on his sword, an inch of blade showing above the scabbard. "Do what?" he asked calmly.

"You-you finished it?" Foster blurted, still staring at the shimmering mirror. "That is what was missing? Another element..." His voice trailed off, and he shifted his gaze to Gwyn, who still held a pale finger out toward Charles.

Abbie looked at each of her companions, putting together what they had already figured out.

"You didn't do it, then?" she asked Foster. "You can't open a portal by yourself."

"Someone would have had to help him," said Charles, not taking his eyes off Gwyn. "Someone with talent in Water magics. Someone who might be connected to you and want you here."

"But... why do they want me here?" she asked. "Gwyn...?"

"Half-elf," said an unfamiliar voice, a bit of a quaver drawing out the words. The voice somehow echoed in the small cabin. Gwyn's eyes widened as he looked past Charles, but the human didn't move, his hand still gripping the sword hilt tightly.

Abbie whirled around and saw that Grandmother Winter's eyes were open. A gnarled hand rose from the bed covers, pointing straight at her. Foster fell to the ground, kneeling with his face to the floor as the temperature in the room dropped abruptly and the fire burned blue white.

"Half-elf," repeated the old Queen, her voice gaining a bit of strength. "He brought you here for betrayal."

The mirror continued to coalesce into a portal until the Queen waved her hand tiredly and the magic dispersed.

"No!" cried Abbie, dashing to the mirror and slapping her hand on it. Nothing happened as she pressed her palm to the frosty glass. "Please! I just want to go home!"

Gwyn made a strange, gasping sound, and Abbie looked up to see him fly backward until he slammed against the wall of the cabin, sticking there like a pinned insect. The old woman struggled to sit up in her bed, her cap askew.

"You will *not* go home," she said to Abbie. "Half-elf." She sounded angry, but her voice was still weak and wobbly with age. Foster kept his face on the floor as Charles slowly turned around to face the Queen, his sword still partially drawn. "Winter, Summer, human, and half-elf—all intruding on my rest."

"Stay there," the Queen added, gesturing to Charles.

Charles didn't move, and Abbie stepped to his side, looking up at him. His eyes looked down at her, but he seemed frozen in place. As she watched, ice crystals grew slowly across his skin.

"*Who* is betraying me?" asked Abbie plaintively, utterly confused. Gwyn gurgled from the wall, and she looked from him to the Queen. "Please don't hurt us!"

"Hurt you?" The old Queen gargled a laugh, ignoring the girl. "Did you bring her here for me, son of Nudd? A tasty treat, with all her wild magic?" She smacked her lips together, a ghastly grin revealing one lone tooth in her mouth. "Trying to curry favor to regain your station?"

Abbie retreated in horror, but the Queen caught her with a swirl of magic, shards of ice surrounding the girl and pulling her closer while Foster whimpered on the floor. Suddenly, the lone window shattered, a dark shape crashing through it. A brown wolf landed, snarling, in the middle of the room.

The Queen released Abbie in surprise, and the girl fell forward to the floor, catching herself with her hands. The wolf stood on its hind legs against Charles, pulling at his cloak with its mouth, its sharp teeth flashing by his neck. Abbie threw her hands out toward her defenseless friend, ice still growing over his body, and knocked the wolf backward with a blast of air. Charles's cloak came free and covered the animal.

The old elven Queen cackled as the animal thrashed under the white fabric, but she remained in the bed, apparently not quite strong enough to rise.

"Wild magic to strengthen me," she muttered, turning gimlet eyes toward the girl once more.

Abbie crossed her arms in front of herself, a shield glyph instinctually forming for protection as the Winter Queen reached out for her again.

The shield momentarily thwarted the Queen's magic, and Abbie quickly strengthened it, expanding a dome of Air to keep Charles and Foster safe as well. Magic smashed harmlessly to the side against the nearly invisible wall she had created as the Queen gargled with rage.

The wolf stopped struggling in the corner and stood up, taller and taller until it looked at Abbie with the familiar face of Nadiene. The wolf wrapped the cloak around her torso, tucked it in tightly, and reached for the fireplace. Outside the window, white shapes moved in the snow—Winter's wolves, closing in.

One white-furred wolf leapt through the window just as Nadiene put her hand on what Abbie had assumed was one of the fireplace tools. The animal growled, gathering its hind quarters to leap at Nadiene as the woman clutched at the rod. The blue-white fire illuminated the object, and Abbie could now see that it was intricately carved and jeweled—certainly not a fireplace poker. Nadiene spun it around and pointed the scepter at the other wolf.

"Be free!" she shouted.

"No!" gasped the Queen, and her attack on Abbie's shield abruptly ended as she directed her anger toward Nadiene. The wolf curled her body around the scepter, shielding her prize, and the Queen's magic slammed her into the wall. "Kill her!" she ordered the Winter wolf, who turned slowly toward Nadiene.

Abbie could feel her grasp on the Air shield weakening, but she didn't know what to do about it. Foster stood up next to her, saying something about tying it off, but she looked at him with unfocused eyes. It was hard to understand what was going on. The scene around her grew blurry, and she couldn't make sense of what he was saying.

As she looked back at him, the mirror on the wall rippled and widened suddenly, expanding like a vertical pool of water. Dark shapes appeared in the bright water, undulating and indiscernible.

Then her father stepped through the mirror into the cabin.

CHAPTER 20

Reunion

ABBIE'S HEART LEAPT at the sight of her father, her shield failing as he stepped fully into the room. He grew larger in her eyes as the old Queen's magic ensnared her again with ice, and he seemed to burn with a fierce light that cast the contents of the cabin into sharp relief. The Queen screeched with fury as Wodan cast a burst of fire toward her, losing her icy grip on the girl as she shielded herself from the flames.

The Winter wolf stood stock still, continuing to stare at Nadiene as she also fell free from the Queen's magic.

"You are free to do as you wish," Nadiene growled at it, and the white wolf cocked its head to the side, confused.

"I said wait!" huffed another voice, smooth as silk. A woman with purple hair wearing a bright blue suit stepped through the Gate, her lime green heels clicking on the stone floor. In the firelight, her shadow loomed larger than anyone else's in the room. "I was *going* to tell you what you were about to walk into, Wodan. Or rather, where," she added, turning slightly to take in the entire cabin, which now felt impossibly crowded.

Abbie stumbled as the Queen's ice magic released her, grabbing hold of Foster for support. He thrust one hand down to the floor, pulling green vines through the seams and up from the earth below the stones.

"Stop!" The old Queen trembled from her bed, covers in disarray as she pointed a gnarled finger toward the younger woman stalking toward her. Still depending on her wolves to save her, the Queen cast billows of thick fog into the room, obscuring everything.

The purple woman sighed theatrically, but her march continued forward. Abbie clutched at Foster, whose eyes searched wildly for a way out.

"We can't leave Charles!" Abbie pleaded, even though she couldn't tell where the big man was standing anymore.

A dark shape loomed on their left, and a bright flame appeared, burning away the unnaturally thick fog.

"Daddy!" Abbie cried as he knelt beside them, fire in his hand.

Wodan pulled his daughter in for a one-armed embrace as he maintained the flame.

"We have to go."

He looked over his shoulder to where the Queen let out an unearthly wail somewhere in the fog.

"I can't leave my friends," Abbie said.

She stood up next to Foster who looked terrified, still controlling and surrounded by a thickening set of vines.

Her father frowned, considering the danger of an angry elven Queen in the room, until the fog abruptly dissipated. Charles fell to his knees, hands catching his weight as he pitched forward on the stone floor, ice falling away from him, and Gwyn tumbled down off the far wall.

Everyone turned toward Grandmother Winter, who stared deeply into the amber eyes of the strange woman with the large shadow. The Cat sat on the edge of the bed, her hand on the side of the Queen's face.

"You will be a good girl now, won't you?" said the Cat.

Tears streamed from the old elf's eyes, but she seemed powerless to resist whatever spell the Cat had cast on her.

Gwyn picked himself up off the ground, only to be stopped by Charles's sword, the tip pressing dangerously into his chest. The Winter elf put up his hands.

"Steady now, Charles," said Gwyn. "Ah, Wodan, so glad you could make it."

Wodan stood, one hand on Abbie, holding her against his side. She was more than content to stay there, her arm secured around his waist. He wore a sword, but he did not draw it. The thieftaker confronted Gwyn while the two wolves continued to face off near the broken window. The storm outside had died down to nothing, and the Cat was doing... *something*... to the Queen.

"Nadiene!" called out Abbie, and the tall wolf flicked her gaze toward her, eyes gleaming gold.

The Winter wolf, still in furred form, whined and jumped out the window. Nadiene sagged a little, clothed only in Charles's cloak wrapped tightly around her like a towel, still clutching the scepter.

"I had hoped to do that myself," said the Cat. "I will take that now, wolf."

She held out her hand, and the jeweled rod jumped toward her, nearly dragging Nadiene along with it.

"No!" She panicked, pulling back hard, the knuckles of both her hands whitening. "The Wolfsbane Scepter should be destroyed!"

"Pfft, that would be a waste," said the Cat. She placed her free hand on the Queen's forehead, and the scepter yanked itself free from Nadiene's grasp and smacked solidly into the

Cat's palm. "Do not worry, wolf. I will not enslave you again. And I spare your life—but leave here at once with your fellow thieftaker and never come back. Nor shall you tell anyone what you saw here."

The Cat's eyes glittered dangerously, her vertical pupils dilating.

Nadiene hesitated, meeting Charles's gaze across the room. He raised an eyebrow and nodded slightly toward Gwyn, whom he still held at sword point.

"Leave him be, ginger," snapped the Cat. "My offer of safe passage through Winter back to your home will not be on the table much longer."

"You can go home," interrupted Abbie, her voice louder than she thought it would be. Everyone turned to look at her, and she wanted to shrink behind her dad, but instead she stepped forward. "Your real home." She pointed at the portal, which was still open on the large mirror.

The big, bearded man gave the Gate a long look. He shook his head. "There is nothing for me there, little one."

"I'll be there," she said, held back from going to his side by her father's grip. "You can stay with us. Right, Dad?"

Wodan's eyebrows shot up, and he looked awkwardly at the human thieftaker. "Ah, well…"

"A kind offer, Abbie," said Charles. "I must refuse. My home is here with her." He grinned at Nadiene, his teeth white against his ruddy beard. The wolf rolled her eyes, and he grudgingly sheathed his sword. Gwyn got to his feet and walked immediately to where the Cat sat on the bed, standing next to her like a guard.

The Cat put a hand on the Winter elf's arm possessively, and he looked down at her with a smile.

"We will take your Deal," said Nadiene, her voice rough. "If the boy Foster is included in it."

"What?" The Cat looked at the young Guardian-in-training and waved a hand dismissively. "Of course. Him too. You must leave now and tell no one. In return, you will receive safe passage, and *I won't kill you here*." Her shadow bristled like a living thing, and Abbie could have sworn it looked like a dragon.

"We have a Bargain," said Nadiene, the Deal magic settling down on them.

She held out her hand to Foster, who still hung back behind Abbie and her father. The greenery he had grown shriveled as he stepped forward slowly.

"You tricked us," Foster said to Gwyn, who raised an elegant white eyebrow in reply. He turned to Abbie and her father who stood tall behind her. "He opened the Gate! He brought you here in the first place! He cannot be trusted!"

Wodan slowly lifted a hand. Gwyn app Nudd did the same as Wodan circled around toward the Cat and the Queen, always facing the rest of the group.

"I was told you had died, Gwyn."

"Obviously, I did not."

"You put my daughter in mortal danger for what purpose?"

"She is alive and well," Gwyn responded calmly, but there was a swell of fear in his eyes.

"Destroy yourselves," croaked the Queen from the side of the room, her voice barely audible. The Cat tsked and whispered in the old elf's ear.

Wodan's hand began to glow with orange light, heating the freezing air in the room and competing with the blue flames on the hearth. "Her life—"

"Stop talking about me like I'm not here!" shouted Abbie, stamping her foot. "Gwyn saved my life." She squirmed out of her father's grasp and stood in between the two men. "Everything is weird right now, but maybe Gwyn didn't betray us. *She* said he was bringing me here for her to eat," she said, pointing at Grandmother Winter, who was shrinking away from the Cat as much as she could, as if a much larger creature were perched on her bed. "But I don't think he did. She attacked him, too."

Abbie put her hands on her hips, facing down her father, and then exclaimed, "Who's that?"

A great bear of a man came through the Gate behind Wodan, followed by another, smaller man, gripping the upper arm of a girl who looked disturbingly familiar. Abbie blinked.

That girl looks just like me! thought Abbie.

"It's a changeling!" breathed Foster, eyes wide.

"Don't get me wrong—this is all very fascinating and heart-warming, or… whatever." The Cat waved a hand dismissively, as if she were wiping away the extraneous emotions from the room. "Close the Gate."

The changeling looked at Wodan for confirmation of the orders, but he narrowed his eyes and shook his head. Another person came through the portal, a woman with long blond hair who swore loudly when she saw where she was.

"Winter's heart?" She put her hands on the two throwing axes she wore on her hips. "I should have known."

Abbie's eyebrows climbed with the swearing, and she filed the new words away for examining at length later.

"Close the Gate!" thundered the purple-haired woman.

The changeling quailed but did nothing. The man holding her arm shook her like a doll. Wodan faced down the Cat.

"It will close the Gate when I tell it to. That's the Deal I made with it."

"Then tell it to close it now. Stop those infernal Hunters from entering!" the Cat screeched as two more people stepped through.

Wodan's hand began to glow with fire, and the Hunters spread through the cabin, their human disguises falling away as they breathed back in the powers that had been stripped away so long ago. There were too many of them to handle, not without danger to the dragon's ongoing plans.

Gwyn held up a slim, white hand and bowed slightly to the Cat. "If I may?"

She nodded, seething. The Queen was slumped over in the bed, eyes closed. Her chest rose and fell with shallow breathing.

"I know this is confusing, Wodan, and I do not have adequate time to explain it, but there has been a change of leadership in Winter. I helped bring your daughter to the Otherworld, yes, but not for *Mab*." He spoke the Winter Queen's name without fear, even though others in the overcrowded room flinched. "The Cat helped me evade the Exile. Faked my death. I have been working for *her* the whole time."

Wodan frowned, holding up his hand to keep the Hunters at bay. "To… *this* end?" He gestured at the cabin and the Queen. "To strike Winter at its center?"

"Exactly, yes, yes. Due to many well-worded Bargains, the dragons, my brethren, have been forced into near extinction," the Cat interrupted, exasperated and trying to stay in control of the situation. "We were once one of the most powerful factions of the Otherworld. Both Summer and Winter sought our counsel and advice. And now—now I live in the stinking world of humans while my—" She stopped talking, snapping her mouth shut, her amber eyes flashing angrily.

Abbie took in the scene with wide eyes. She had stepped to the side to where Foster was, and the two youngsters stood back to back, holding hands.

"The Queen is at her weakest, and the changeling opened the portal to the seat of her power." Gwyn gestured at Abbie, who flinched. "As you know, half-elves are not held by the Accords, which is why they are never allowed to live. The Queens know they can disrupt the Balance. Under the Accords, no one may open a Gate to a throne room. Except for one little, inconsequential loophole."

He smiled like a shark.

"Close the Gate," said the Cat. Her voice cracked and deepened as her shadow began to grow, dark wings against the walls. "Get out! Winter's power will soon be mine!"

Even as she spoke, ice crystals began to form inside the cabin, coating the walls and startling the people inside.

Charles grabbed Foster's hand, his eyes on the sharply dressed woman on the other side of the room as a blast of freezing wind sprang forth from her. "Just as well that I hate long goodbyes. Be well, Abbie."

She looked up at him, a little confused, but still waved.

Nadiene nodded to her, a silent farewell. She pulled the cloak over her head and dropped to the floor, emerging in her canine form.

Foster blurted, "Goodbye!" as Charles tugged him toward the door, and Abbie reached out for him with a fierce hug, broken up as her father pulled her away.

"There's no time," Wodan hissed, fear swelling inside him at the dragon's control over the Winter Queen's magic.

The trio escaped into the wintery landscape beyond the cabin, and the sudden disappearance of her friends seemed, to Abbie, much more important than whatever was going on with the Queen, or Winter, or even dragons.

"Close the Gate!" boomed the Cat in a gravelly voice, and Wodan dropped his hand to his sword as the cabin began to creak and shake.

There was no time for further goodbyes, let alone any other words. The Hunters who had made it through the portal followed the example set by the thieftakers, running out of the cabin toward their new freedom, and Wodan walked backward toward the Gate, holding Abbie's hand so tightly it hurt.

"Close it behind us," he said to his daughter's changeling.

Abbie was pulled through the mirror, her last glimpse of the Otherworld the Cat's enormous dragonesque shadow overtaking the room until a wide smile of sharp teeth was all that was left.

CHAPTER 21

The Fae Child

ABBIE STUMBLED ON the other side of the Gate, her father's hand the only thing keeping her upright as her eyes adjusted to the darkness of the night. Behind them, the portal closed without a sound and they were suddenly and utterly alone.

Wodan stepped through the ring of white mushrooms, looking around the clearing as best he could. The sudden rush of magic in the Otherworld, coupled with its equally abrupt loss when he'd stepped back through the Gate, was disorienting. Everything was quiet, and after a moment of stillness, a cricket began to chirp.

Abbie took a deep breath. "Where's Mom?"

"Back home. With Sammy." Wodan looked down at his daughter. "She doesn't think that you've been gone."

The little girl nodded thoughtfully. "Because of the other girl. The changeling." She hugged him tightly. "How did you know to look for me?"

He knelt and swept her into his arms. "Because I... I'm an elf, Abbie. I knew that thing wasn't you almost as soon as I saw it."

"I know," she said into his shoulder. "Foster—he explained everything to me." She sighed, upset at how quickly they had been forced to say goodbye.

"He sounds like he was a good friend to you. I will always be grateful that you found good people to help you, and that you are such a brave and smart girl, Abbie." Wodan kissed her hair, and Abbie put her arms around his neck. He stood up, carrying her easily as he walked back toward their home.

"Will they be okay?" she asked. "My friends?"

He was quiet for a little while. "I think so. The Bargain they struck with the Cat—the woman who neutralized the Queen—should see them safely into Summer again."

"Good."

Abbie yawned sleepily, resting her head on her father's shoulder until they reached their home and he opened the back door. She popped up and he set her down, Sammy immediately swarming her legs and jumping up on her.

She fell to her knees to hug the ecstatic Jack Russell terrier. "Did you miss me, boy?"

He whined and licked her face in reply, and she giggled.

"Dan?" Fiona's voice called out from the other room. "Where's Abbie? I woke up and she was gone!"

"Mom!" Abbie leapt to her feet and darted into the living room. "Mom! I'm back!"

"Oh, thank God," said her mother, nearly falling back into the couch as Abbie tackled her. "You cannot leave the house at night, young woman!"

"I won't ever again," promised Abbie, tears in her eyes as she hugged Fiona.

Wodan watched closely, stepping forward to help his wife free of Abbie's fierce hug. Fiona looked exhausted and frail, and Abbie frowned as she looked up at her mother.

"Are you okay?"

"Just a little tired," promised Fiona. "It *is* the middle of the night after all. You are going back to bed right now, Abbie."

"But I—"

"Probably a good idea," added Wodan. "We can talk in the morning."

"But—" Abbie couldn't imagine sleeping now. "Everything is *different* now!"

"No buts, young lady," said Fiona. She looked up at her husband for help. "Can you get her back to bed? I just… I feel so tired."

"You need your rest, too," he agreed, bending to kiss Fiona on the forehead. With the changeling gone, she would recover her lost vitality, though it would take some time.

Sammy followed Wodan and Abbie up the stairs, sitting on her feet as she brushed her teeth, then hopping into bed with her. No one stopped him, and he snuggled under the covers until just his nose was sticking out.

"Dad?" Abbie looked up at Wodan from the pillow, narrowing her eyes.

"Yes?"

"You know you don't look the same anymore."

He touched the tips of his ears. "Ah."

"Mom's gonna notice eventually."

"I suppose she will. We will work it out." Wodan offered a half smile. "When she is stronger."

"Okay."

"Goodnight, Abbie."

"Dad?"

He paused, just about to turn away and close the door, and looked back at her. "Yes?"

"I'm a half-elf."

"I know."

"You don't have to worry about me anymore. 'Cause I'm home. And I can do this."

Abbie sat up in bed, concentrating, and Wodan watched in wonder as she drew a glyph in the air. It shimmered and a hardened shield of Air wove around her.

He didn't know what to say. Was *this* why half-elves were forbidden? By their nature as creatures of both worlds they existed outside of the bounds of the ancient Bargains made between elves and humans. A half-elf appeared to have the strengths of both species, a strength that circumvented the Accords. After a moment, he realized his mouth was open, and he closed it.

The shield dissipated and Abbie sighed tiredly, snuggling back down into her pillows. "Goodnight, Dad."

"Goodnight, Abbie," he breathed. Her room seemed to glow with motes of light, the use of her magic stirring up what the humans would call "fairy dust." After a few moments, the fragments of magic faded, leaving just the nightlight to illuminate the bedroom.

Wodan closed the door and sat on the floor inside Abbie's room. He watched her sleep until his eyes closed with exhaustion.

When the sun rose, it found the Brown family reunited, and everything was as it should be—and somehow even *more* than before, in all the best ways.

THE END

ACKNOWLEDGMENTS

Writing a book has been a dream of mine since I was a child. Writing *this* book has been a rollercoaster, and one I couldn't have ridden out without the love and support of my family and friends.

First, I must thank Ty, my husband, for always being there for me. When I didn't want to keep going, you encouraged me to take the time I needed to get it right. You've worked long hours and come home to find that the dishes weren't done and dinner wasn't made, but you didn't complain (much). I honestly never could have come this far without your love and support. Thank you, Ty. I love you more than I can express in words.

To my parents, Jim and Anne: you nurtured and sheltered me and fed my creative side for the first eighteen years of my life. Mom, you taught me how to read and write, and you let me write one of my first "research papers" as a story when I was six, which really kicked this whole "novelist" thing off in the first place. Thank you so much for supporting my creative endeavors.

I want to thank my kids, Owen, Sophie, Olivia, and Logan, for not distracting me *too* much while I drafted this story. And for providing me examples every day of how kids approach problems and communicate their feelings. There is a little bit of each of you in the character of Abbie. Much love forever. I dedicated *Fae Child* to you because I hope that one day, when you are on your own adventures, you are as brave and strong as Abbie. You will discover inside you what it is that makes you special and unique, and when you do, nothing will be able to stop you. Also, remember to brush your teeth.

To my author crew I met throughout this lengthy process—Michael Haase, Tahani Nelson, Ferd Crôtte, Regina McMenomy, Deborah Munro, and so many others—thank you for your encouragement and support. And double thanks to Michael, because without your crucial beta read, I absolutely never would have made it this far. Never ever. In fact, take another helping of thanks, Michael. The Writing Bloc family is awesome!

Thank you to *each and every one* of my friends and family who preordered *Fae Child*, and thank you to the people who preordered who didn't even know me. I was blown away every time one of you took a chance on me and my little story. Because of you and your support, *Fae Child* grew from a one-sentence idea in my head to the book you now hold in your hands.

Much thanks to Inkshares for providing a place for creators to interface directly with their readers, and for being the reason we are all here today, reading the acknowledgments in the back of my first novel.

Aliana Wong, my cover artist, thank you so much for all the work you put into my cover for me. It is breathtaking, and I can't imagine using anything different. Find her online at www.alianawong.com.

Lastly, I want to thank my friends from TheHolo.Net—Christin, Charley, Geoff, Vince, James, Jenny, Andrew, Andrew, and everyone else. The unforgiving crucible of Star

Wars fan fiction is where I honed my craft, and each of you have strengthened my writing in ways I can't even describe. There would be no book today if I hadn't been writing daily with you all for so many years. Without Jenny, there *really* wouldn't be a book, as she's the one who got me involved with Inkshares in the first place.

Most importantly, don't give up on your dreams.

GRAND PATRONS

DJ Breslin

Jacqui Castle

James & Anne Connell

Ferd Crôtte

Deborah Munro

Candice Robertson

Frank M. Root

Johnny Johnson

J. Graham Jones

INKSHARES